DIRTY IRISH

MIA CLARK

Cherrylily Publishing

CONTENTS

Foreword   vii
Description   ix

1. Introduction   1
2. Grace   9
3. Dare   13
4. Grace   19
5. Dare   29
6. Grace   37
7. Dare   43
8. Grace   49
9. Dare   53
10. Grace   59
11. Dare   65
12. Grace   73
13. Dare   77
14. Grace   83
15. Dare   87
16. Grace   89
17. Dare   93
18. Grace   97
19. Dare   103
20. Grace   111
21. Dare   117
22. Grace   119
23. Dare   125
24. Grace   135
25. Dare   141
26. Grace   147
27. Grace   157

28. Dare   163
29. Dare   169

VALENTINE'S AND CHILL (TEASER)

1. Ally   177
2. James   183

A Note from Mia   187
About the Author   193

Dirty Irish
ARC Version

Written by Mia Clark

FOREWORD

Join my VIP readers list and get free books, bonus scenes, extra exclusive content, and more. You'll also be the first to know about new releases, sales, and special giveaways.
Cherrylily.com/Mia
You can also find me on Facebook for more sneak peeks and updates here:
Facebook.com/MiaClarkWrites

And you can find all of my books on Amazon, including my bestselling Stepbrother With Benefits series!
All of Mia Clark's Books

DESCRIPTION

I just want to be naughty for one night of my life.
I think I'd be really good at it...

I need to escape. I'm a bad girl trapped in a good girl's body. Perfect grades, star volleyball player, lead in the drama club. I know it'll lead to a great career.

But I need more.

Just one night. In Ireland. On St. Patrick's Day. Thousands of miles away from anyone who knows me.

That's how I meet Dare Mackenzie.

With fire in his emerald eyes, sinful promises on his lips. And an accent as intoxicating as the darkest stout. He keeps saying I'm too sweet, too innocent, too good.

I *dare* you, Dare Mackenzie. Just try and call me sweet and innocent again!

Sweet? Tasting, maybe.

Innocent? Good girls like that don't do what I'm about to do...

After tonight you'll swim the Atlantic for another taste.

It's not like it matters. We'll never see each other again...

...Right?

INTRODUCTION

I just want to be naughty for once in my life. I think I'd be really good at it...

Now's as good a time as ever, right? I've been planning this for months. Meticulously going over every detail, each possible outcome, until I finally came up with a solution to, well, everything.

My good girl tendencies die hard, apparently. I'm a "bad girl" work in progress. It's fine. I can do this!

"Melanie," I say for the millionth time. "I'm really sorry but I just won't be able to make it to volleyball practice this weekend. I know the squad had a whole St. Patrick's Day thing planned, but I promised my mom I'd come home. It's kind of a big deal for her since she likes to celebrate our Irish heritage, so..."

A half-truth. My mom likes to mention every now and then that her great-grandfather came over from Ireland, but that's about it. We've never done anything for St. Patrick's Day except the occasional corned beef dinner.

"Grace, you're going to miss out on so much fun!" Melanie says for the billionth time. "I know it's not the same as a frat party, but we were going to go out for green rootbeer floats after. Wouldn't that be awesome?"

"Oh, yeah, of course!" I say, trying to sound as cheery as possible. "Those frats can get a little too rowdy, too. Don't want to get into any trouble."

"I know, right! I'm so glad you agree. It's been really nice having you on the squad, Grace. You're a great example for the other girls and I know you'll do a good job of leading everyone once I graduate. I really appreciate you. I just want you to know that, alright?"

And... that makes me feel like a piece of shit, but what can you do? My plan's already in motion and I can't back out now. I mean, technically I *can*, but I'm not going to. I'm a bad girl work in progress, remember? Bad girls don't just cave every time they feel an ounce of remorse for what they're about to do, or what they've already done, or... I don't know.

I don't think they do, at least? I'm still trying to figure this one out.

"Well, I've got to finish packing, so... good luck, Melanie."

"Thanks! You too, Grace. Byeeee~!"

I hang up the phone only to immediately receive another call. This one will be tougher to deal with, but I can do this. I've prepared for this. You've got this, Grace! Go go go!

"Hey, Mom," I say, answering my phone.

"Hey, Gracie," my mom says. "I know you won't be able to

2

make it home this weekend, but your dad and I are doing a corned beef dinner and everything was on sale so I bought more than we could ever eat. I'm going to save you some, alright? How's volleyball going? You said you're doing extra training this weekend?"

"Yup," I say, nodding quietly into my phone for all the good it does me. "The squad's going to do a sort of St. Patrick's Day themed training and everyone's going out for green rootbeer floats after."

This is the truth. It's just not *my* truth. It's not the entire truth.

"Oh, fun," my mom says, a smile in her voice. "I'm sure there's a few big parties going on too, huh?"

"I mean, probably," I say, noncommittal. "You know I don't really do that kind of thing, though."

"I know. You're a good girl, Gracie. I used to worry more. I wasn't sure if you'd be a wild teenager, but you were always good. Even now, too. Your father and I are really proud of you and we trust you so much. I'm not saying that you should do anything irresponsible, but if you're careful and safe and you happen to end up at a party where people are drinking, I just want you to know that we trust you and you can always call us no matter what."

"I haven't really ever been to a party," I admit to her. "If I did, I wouldn't drink a lot, Mom. I'm not legal yet, and we aren't supposed to drink during volleyball season, either. We all agreed not to."

"Well, sure," my mom says, probably grinning at me as we speak. "I know how college is, honey. I was a college student at one point, too. I know, that's hard to believe, but it's true. I guess I just want you to know that there'll be no judgment from me or your father if you do happen to end up a little buzzed or tipsydoodle or whatever you kids call it these days. If you ever need us to drive there and get you, just give us a call."

"Mom, you're two hours away," I remind her.

"That's if your father goes the speed limit. If you need us, I think we can cut it down to an hour, max."

"Mom!" I say, laughing. "You were doing so well with the 'be responsible' speech before."

"Always go the speed limit, too, Gracie. Don't be like your father. He's such a bad boy."

"Oh, sure," I say, rolling my eyes. "Right. Of course he is."

My mom smiles through the phone, a lilt of laughter shared between us. "Just remember to take some time for yourself, too. Volleyball is important, and so are your grades, and so is drama club, and so are a lot of other things, but sometimes we need to be a little selfish and enjoy ourselves. That's all."

"I know, Mom," I say, quiet. "Um, can I let you go for now? I was about to go study for a little. I've got a big exam in a couple weeks."

"Sure, honey. You and the girls have a great weekend, alright? Call me later if you can."

"I will, Mom. Thank you. I can't wait to try the corned beef dinner. Definitely save me some."

"I'm going to make it green!" she says, giddy. And then, "Bye, Gracie."

4

I take one final, deep breath before saying, "Bye, Mom." And then I hang up my phone, put it on airplane mode, and stuff it in my pocket.

I step out of a quiet alcove in the airport and join the hustle and bustle of everyone else traveling during a holiday weekend. I'm glad I got here early because this place is absolutely packed. I dodge soon-to-be passengers in a rush, weaving left and right with my stuffed backpack and carry-on duffel bag. It's the same stuff I bring with me when we go on overnight trips for volleyball games, except without any of my volleyball gear this time.

A few minutes later and I'm there, standing outside of gate C34.

"This is our final boarding call for the flight leaving to Dublin, Ireland," a calm woman calls over the intercom. "Please make your way to the front of gate C34 if you're going to Dublin, Ireland. Thank you."

I pull my slightly wrinkled ticket from my pocket and hold it tight between my fingers and thumb. Joining the line to board the plane to Dublin, I anxiously look out the floor to ceiling glass windows at the plane outside. The livery's all green, with a picture of a four-leaf clover emblazoned on the tail.

Before I know it, I'm at the front of the line. Also the end of the line. I'm the last person to board today. The woman at the ticket scanner looks up and smiles at me as I hand her my ticket.

"First time traveling alone?" she asks.

I nod, meek. Bad girl work in progress, remember? I'm working on it!

"St. Patrick's Day weekend in Dublin is a great first solo trip," she says, excited for me. "You're going to love it. Go and see the parade if you can. It's a blast!"

I smile, gaining a little more courage with each passing second. It *will* be a blast, won't it? I mean, this is what I've been preparing for for, oh, I don't know, the past six months? I don't quite have that bad girl spontaneity down yet, but my good girl tendencies really pulled through with this one. I don't think I have to be solely one or the other. I can be a little bit of both sometimes, you know?

"Thank you," I say. "I'm really excited about it. I want to go to the zoo, too."

Yup. I just said that. I'm the only girl in the world excited about going to the Dublin zoo during St. Patrick's Day weekend, I'm sure.

"The zoo's great!" she says, laughing. "Should be quiet this weekend so you'll have it all to yourself. Have fun, sweetie."

She hands me back my ticket, having scanned it awhile ago, and I stride down the hallway to my waiting plane. A flight attendant greets me with a smile and a hello as I board.

"You should still have some room in the overhead compartments for your bag, but you might have to put it way in the back," he says. "Do you want me to help you find a spot?"

"Nah, I got this," I say.

See? Bad girl!

Totally.

Maybe not.

I do find a spot for my carry-on, though.

Just remember to take some time for yourself, my mom said. *Sometimes we need to be a little selfish and enjoy ourselves.*

Not sure this is what she had in mind, but hopefully she'll find it cute and funny when I tell her after I get back...

GRACE

My first day here was a blur of catching up on some sleep, being a huge tourist and gaping over every little thing, wandering through crowds of St. Patrick's, or I guess St. *Paddy's*, Day revelers, and also oh my gosh the zoo, you guys!

They had the cutest little red pandas that kind of looked like big raccoons except super adorable and cuddly and silly. One of them tried to pounce on a rock while standing on two feet and stretching his little paws high up in the air.

I died of a cuteness overload right then. But don't worry, I'm back! I've been revived by the frantic St. Paddy's Day celebrations going on.

The first day was wonderful and exciting, but this second day? The *actual* St. Paddy's Day? That's today and I'm one-hundred percent prepared to take full advantage of it.

Or I'm *trying*, at least. I may have underestimated just

how excited Irish people get about St. Patrick's Day. Barricades block off the streets, all traffic coming to a complete halt as everyone prepares for the parade. I'm still trying to get my bearings, plus my phone doesn't work very well here, so it's a bit of an adventure, you know? I know the streets that I should be heading to, but it's just a little hard to get to them, plus I have to figure out where I am and where I'm going every few blocks, so, um...

The river, though. I know that one. River Liffey. If I follow the road alongside the river to the bridge up ahead then I should be at a good spot to see the parade. I would be if it were a little less crowded, but I'm tall enough to at least see over some people's heads so I think I'll be fine.

I maneuver my way down the tiny sidewalk next to the river down below, only a small stone wall between me and the riverside cliff. I peek over every now and then, watching the deep blue water meander slowly out to Dublin Bay. I got to see a little more of that yesterday when I checked out *Dun Laoghaire* Harbour, and I have no idea how to pronounce that but it was a definite highlight of my trip so far.

Dublin is a beautiful city, packed with history and wonderful architecture. I think that's my good girl tendency speaking again, but I did hop into a small "old man's pub" as they call it (literally someone told me that's what they call it) and ordered a pint of Guinness because that seemed like the proper Irish thing to do.

It wasn't even that bad! The stout was good, but that's not what I meant. I'm of legal drinking age in Ireland, so drinking is, um... not a bad girl thing to do here? I don't know. I just had one with some thick cut chips while listening to a raucous little band play a few classic Celtic songs with a contemporary twist.

No dancing yet, though. I don't know if I'm ready for that.

At any rate, the river. The walkway alongside it. Me. I'm heading to the parade, just minding my own business, when suddenly I hear something barking down below.

I can't go very fast, or very far, so I stop for a few and peek over the small stone wall again to see what's barking up at me. And, oh my gosh, the most adorable little family of otters is playing in the water right below me. Mama Otter splashes her little babies and the two babies swim in frenzied circles, chasing each other. Papa Otter swims off to the side, barking loudly at everyone, but not really doing much to stop it. I don't know if he's cheering them on, or telling them to stop being so feckin' wild, or whatever else Irish otters might say.

It's cute, it's adorable, and I want to take a picture. I reach for my pocket to grab my phone, but as soon as I pull it out someone jostles me from the side. My phone starts to teeter in my hand, on the verge of toppling over the wall and falling into the water. Without thinking, I reach for it fast with my other hand, but, um...

So, the stone wall alongside the river's edge isn't exactly the tallest, and there's a long ways to go if I fall over.

Which, you know, I'm doing. I'm about to do. I have my phone firmly held in both hands, so that's safe for all the good it'll do me, but my upper body is decidedly about to crash over the stone wall, bringing my lower body along with it, and I sure hope those otters like company because I'll be joining them any second now...

Someone wraps their arms around my waist and hoists me back over the stone wall before I take a dive into the water. I stand there, eyes and mouth wide open, gaping at what just almost happened.

As if he's the hero from one of my drama club plays, a brown-haired bad boy with streaks of dark red in his hair eyes me up and down, takes my now free hand (the other gripping tight to my phone), and spins me in a circle.

"Looks like you're doing fine," he says with a nod of approval followed by a devilish wink. "Next time you want to take a dip in the river let me know. I've a better spot to jump in."

DARE

This girl's a real looker, yeah? The problem's that I saved her life and now she's looking at me like I'm the devil in a church and I'll be the sole reason God smites the entire place with a flashy bolt of thunder and lightning.

Might not have actually saved her life. A dip in the river never killed anyone, though I'm not too sure I'd want to tumble into Liffey wearing what she's got on. It's a little chill out for it, too. Maybe in a few months when the summer sets us up with a bit of heat, and then I'd spend every waking moment trying to convince her to put on her skimpiest swimsuit and join me for some alone time near the water if you get what I mean.

This flower of a girl stares up at me with a hint of that summer heat in her eyes and a scowl curling her lips. I stare right back at her, tossing a bit of the old shimmer and shine her way, a smirk and a wink along with it.

She's tall enough, I'll give her that. Menacing? Nah, sorry, lass, not so much. The chic copper red bomber jacket she's got on, sleeves pulled up to her elbows, almost looks like she means business, but those cute little dimples that she couldn't hide to save her life ruin the mood. The multi-green and white flannel shirt tied about her waist isn't helping. It's like she's trying so hard to look like she's rough around the edges, but her edges are satin soft and smooth to the touch.

I glance down a sec at her tight jeans, ripped near the knees, then back up to that same beautiful scowl of hers. Oi, I'm in trouble with this one. I can feel it deep already.

"Did ye jus' spin me 'round like a top?" she asks, a fake Irish accent dripping from her kissable lips.

Oh, the things I'd do if you'd just stop with the scowling, gorgeous...

"Where ya from, love?" I ask her.

She flinches like I've wounded her pride, then she stands up to her full height, a full ten centimeters shorter than me even if she's lifting chin up as high as the sun.

"Here," she says, lying her arse off. "Ireland."

"You got the Ireland right," I say, grinning at her. "Too thick with the rest of the words, though. Trying too hard, love. Just ease up and let it come natural."

"I'll have you know that I've done plenty of English, Scottish, and Irish accents in more plays than you can count and I've never had any complaints."

"Aye, I'm sure you have," I say, laughing. "An American girl, eh? Interesting. Real interesting."

"I'm... I'm not..." she says, sputtering.

"I'd bet my Uncle Mickey's gravestone you're American," I tell her.

"That's a little rude, don't you think?" she asks. "What would your uncle think of that?"

"I dunno. You wanna come with me and go find him? We can ask him in person. He hasn't passed on yet so I'm sure he wouldn't mind, though. Who needs a gravestone if you're not dead, yeah?"

"You're very strange," she says to me.

"You're the one who nearly fell into the river," I tell her. "Chasing your phone, too. Typical American girl, eh?"

"*And* you're very rude!" she adds. "I... I wanted to take a picture of the otters. Not that it's any of your business."

I sidle up alongside her and peek over the stone wall towards the river.

"Aye, those're otters alright," I say. "You still want your picture, American girl?"

"I have a name," she says, huffing at me.

"Take your picture quick and then we'll do introductions."

With a glare, as if she can't be bothered with what I think but she still wants this picture, she leans over the stone wall and snaps a quick pic with her phone. So as to be a true gentleman, I slide my palms on her hips and steady her so she won't go accidentally jumping in again any time soon.

"Um, excuse you?" she says, tilting her head sideways and staring down at my hands.

"Yeah, you're welcome, beautiful," I say, taking my hands back.

"I have a name."

"Do ya? Mine's Dare. Nice to meet you--" I'll let her finish that one. I hold my hand out for her to shake, but she stares at it like she's never seen a handshake in her entire life.

"I need to go," she says, looking down the way. "I wanted to get closer to the parade before it starts and you've held me up long enough."

"Yeah?" I counter. "That's how you're gonna do me. I rescue you from certain doom and I can't even get your name? Huh!"

"I would have been fine," she says, unsure of herself. "I... I would have, um... has anyone ever told you that you have very green eyes? It's distracting."

"Is it now?" I ask, flashing a bright smile at her. "If you think that's distracting, wait until--"

"Nope! No, thank you!" she adds, pulling her eyes away from mine. "Grace. That's my name. There. Are you happy?"

"Yeah, I am," I tell her. "Lovely name for a beautiful girl and I'm glad to know it."

Her cheeks burn red, matching the color of her lips for half a moment before outshining them completely. She stares me in the eyes again, looking close at what is or isn't, or what could be. I'll be arsed if I know what's going on between us but I'm taking a liking to this American girl named Grace and I'd like to learn more about her.

Which, why in the hell not?

"You use that line on all the American girls, I bet?" she

says, a hint of a question, but more like she doesn't want a true answer.

"You want the truth?" I ask. "Aye, technically I have, but you're the first I've met, so you're it."

"What? I don't believe you."

"Aye, lady Grace. You're the only American girl for me. I fell for you right away, or if we're being accurate you fell for me right quick and I caught you. That's how it works, yeah?"

"You're never going to stop with saying you saved me, are you?"

"Are you going to admit I saved you?" I counter.

"Maybe..." she says, a glimmer in her eyes and a grin fast on her lips. "But only if I see you again. Which I won't, because I'm going to find a new way to see the parade. It looks like the sidewalk's filled up this way. It was nice to meet you, Dare, but I really need to go now. Thank you for... for helping me take a picture of those cute otters. That's it. Nothing else."

"You're more than welcome, Grace, but I'm going to do you one even better than that," I tell her.

"Are you now?" she asks, one cute little brow rising up to the sky.

"Aye, but you're not in the right clothes." I look her up and down, trying to spot more green, but all she's got on her is that bit of dark and light green flannel tied about her waist. "We're gonna need to find you more green, love."

"Um..."

"If you're quick, we can duck down here and get you

sorted into something better," I say, gesturing towards an alleyway across the street. "You ready?"

"Um, what?"

"Don't suppose you're good at acting, are ya?" I ask with a smirk. "Not that fake Irish accent acting like before."

"I've been in the drama club since high school," she says, hands on her hips. "I don't mean to have an ego about it or anything, but I know a thing or two about acting, you Irish scoundrel."

"Oi! Irish scoundrel, eh? I like that."

"You called me 'American girl' so I thought I should at least get to call you something back."

"If you want to do it like my ma, you can always add in my family name. Give it a whirl, Grace. It's Mackenzie."

"I know *quite* a lot about acting, Dare Mackenzie!" she says, a half grin on her lips quickly replaced by a fierce grimace as she holds to her character, hands tight to her hips like I've done her wrong.

"Keep that up and I'll want to kiss you before the hour's over," I tell her, smirking fast.

"Um, what!"

"This way, Grace. Hurry it up or we'll miss it."

I tug on her hand and pull her across the street through the gathering crowd. Once we're in the tight alleyway everyone clears away. We make a run for it, Grace following fast on my heel as I lead her to a place a few blocks away where my mate has a flat.

GRACE

Every single part of me says this is a bad idea. Except isn't that the whole point of my weekend getaway?

Be the bad girl, Grace. Give in to a little temptation. Um, not too much temptation! Calm down, girl. Your newfound Irish stud might be, well, very studly in a cozy and friendly sort of way. That makes him sound completely unattractive, doesn't it? That's sort of what I'm going for, though. Temper expectations, remove temptation, and be bad for the sake of it, not just in the cliché sort of sleeping around kind of way.

If I were the sleeping around sort of bad girl, Dare Mackenzie would hit every spot possible, though. And... thinking about him hitting *every spot possible* is making my mind go wild when I really don't want it to.

This isn't about that! That's... that's not what this weekend was supposed to be about.

Just because I want to be a bad girl for the weekend doesn't mean I'm just going to sleep around with whatever attractive Irish guy comes my way. In fact, I'm not planning on sleeping around with anyone. I can be my own brand of bad girl, which doesn't involve sex whatsoever.

There. Now that we've gotten that out of the way...

Dare looks back to make sure I'm still following behind him. He knows his way around the city, apparently, but not the regular streets and roads. He ducks and dodges through different side streets and alleyways, leading me on a wild chase through the lesser known side paths of Dublin.

His eyes stare into mine, almost like he can see right through me. Bright green, brighter still whenever a stray ray of sunshine catches them just the right way. His tousled, short cropped but slightly curly hair shifts as he moves, a stray hand brushing it back every now and then, sending my heart fluttering with passionate demands that I refuse to give in to.

Nope. Not today, heart. Bad girls don't fall in love at first sight, either. Maybe bad girls don't fall in love at all. I'll never find out since I'll only be one for the weekend.

Dare's definitely not the kind of guy that a good girl would fall in love with, either. Yes, he seems charming enough, and he did save me from falling into the river, but there's something about him that makes me think he'd charm the pants off of me if I gave him half a chance, and then he'd charm his way into a lot of pantsless trouble right afterwards.

Tricky. That's what we'll call this. He's the type of boy your mother warned you about, because while he may seem deceptively sweet, it's likely all a ruse for the dirty, naughty things he wants to see if he can convince you into later.

Basically the worst kind of bad boy. The one who refuses to admit he's a bad boy.

Ugh. If I didn't know better I'd think I were in trouble or something.

"Grace, you alright?" he asks, peeking back around a corner he just turned around.

I nearly crash into him, but he sweetly holds out a hand and steadies me by my hip before I can tumble to the cobblestone alley. Sweet, yes. Or completely planned! I know where your hands want to roam, Dare Mackenzie...

I'm totally on to you, you Irish scoundrel.

I eyeball him up and down, real evil and insinuating. "I'm perfectly fine," I tell him. "You can remove your hand from my person now, sir!"

"Sir! Ha!" He laughs as he slides his hand up my arm and caresses his palm against my cheek. "You're cute when you're mad, Grace. Are all American girls like that?"

Without realizing it, I lean into his hand. He teases a finger back along my cheek bone and brushes a stray strand of hair behind my ear. I smile at him without realizing it, my baby blue eyes fully entranced with his emerald green ones, cloudless summer skies meeting countryside and clovers.

And then I snap myself out of it. Bad, Grace! Cut it out!

I snatch his hand and slide it away, putting it back where it belongs; setting it firmly at his side. He grins at me, his fingertips pressing lightly against mine as I pull my hand away.

"You're too charming," I tell him. "Stop it. Be good."

"Aye, I want to be good for you, Grace, but you make it mighty hard when you look at me that way."

"I looked at you in no such way," I inform him, stern. "I'm fine with a little wild, bad girl fun, but only insofar as it doesn't involve you and me naked in a bed. That's it! That's all that's going to happen, meaning it's not going to happen. So if you thought you'd just lure me away from the parade in an attempt to seduce me, well... you've got the wrong impression of me, Dare Mackenzie."

"Oi, shouldn't have told you my surname, eh?" he says, laughing. "Imagine I'll never hear the end of it. Do me a fair trade and tell me yours, Grace?"

"My last name?" I ask, head tilted to the side.

"Aye?"

"Turner," I say.

"Grace Turner," Dare says, tasting my name on his lips and licking them after. "Beautiful, just like you."

"Stop with the charm!" I say, playfully smacking his chest.

"I want to kiss you, Grace Turner," he says, pulling my hand back to his chest, pressing my palm against his tight muscles hidden beneath shirt and cloth.

"You're never going to kiss me, Dare Mackenzie. Not in a million years."

"Aye, not yet," he says. "I want you to *want* to kiss me, too. Just letting you know where my intentions lie."

"And what exactly are your intentions?" I ask. "Did you pull me away so you could try to seduce me in this alley?

Because I'm not about that, and if that's your plan, well... I'll be leaving now."

"Ha! Nah. Right up these steps. Careful, Grace. Be quick about it, though. We haven't got much time. You can leave your things here. We'll come back for them later."

By steps, he means the tiniest set of iron-wrought stairs I've ever seen. They cling to the side of the building like their lives depend on it, barely enough room on each for the balls of our feet. Dare climbs them all without hesitation, swift, like he's some sort of mountain ram. I hold tight to the railing, tiptoeing up the steps as slow as can be. When I nearly reach the top, he holds his hand out to me.

I take his hand in mine and he pulls me up the rest of the way. We rest for barely half a second on this small landing outside a teeny door before Dare creaks the door open and ducks inside. With my hand still in his, he pulls me inside.

Thankfully the inside is much more spacious than the outside. Not by much, though. A small studio apartment greets us, with a twin bed tucked away in the corner and a TV and loveseat against the opposite wall. A tiny door opens into a bathroom across from the bed, with another small closed door near the loveseat.

"Oh, of course," I say with a groan. "Your apartment?"

"Nah, it's my mate's flat," he says. "Asked her if I could keep some things in her closet and she should have what I wanted to get for you, so we're making a quick stopover and then we'll be off."

"Your... mate...?" I say, trying to figure this out. Friend, right? But he said she's a she, so is that like... "You have a girlfriend?"

"What, Shannon? Nah, she's me mate, Grace. Friend, yeah?"

"And you just store things in her flat?"

"Aye, why not?"

"Have you ever had sex with her?" I ask.

"You sure ask a lot of questions, eh?" he counters. "Maybe some people have sex with their female mates, but I'm not one of 'em. Calm yourself, Grace Turner. Nothing of the sort's going on 'round here."

And without further ado, after fishing around in the closet for who knows what, Dare pulls out the most St. Patrick's Day green dress I've ever seen. I don't think it would be possible to wear this on any other day of the year, that's how perfectly green it is. He holds it out in his hands, a proud grin tugging at his lips, eyes smiling at me just as much as the rest of him.

"Here ya go," he says. "Try her on, yeah?"

"Excuse me?"

"Don't know much about dress sizes, but you and Shannon look a pair so I think she'll fit you."

"And why am I putting on this dress?" I ask, clarifying. "What's wrong with what I have on?"

"It doesn't fit the day, don't you think?" he says. "Nothing wrong with it. I like the cute little attempt at looking like a bad girl with those rips at your knees and the bomber jacket. Flannel tied about your waist is nice, too. Good touch, Grace.

Won't work for what I had in mind, though. You don't like dresses?"

"I like dresses just fine, but... I mean, um..."

He puts the dress in my confused hands, then searches through the closet for more. Oh gosh, what have I gotten myself into? I half expect him to pull out a pair of stripper heels and a bright green bonnet or something. But, no, instead he takes out a green vest and a silly hat with a shamrock on it.

"You wanna trade?" he asks, showing me the vest. "Think you'd look prettier in the dress than me, though."

I laugh. I can't help it. Ugh. Just the mental image this tousle-haired, emerald-eyed, Irish sex bomb in a dress, is, um...

Shoot. I just admitted he's a sex bomb, didn't I? Nope. I take it back! The rest is fine but that part is completely, one-hundred percent factually inaccurate.

Mmhmm...

"I don't know where you expect me to change," I tell him. "I'm not changing in front of you."

"Nah, you take the bathroom," he says, nodding across the room. "I'll change out here. Not much to it for me. Just gonna shift some things around, tuck the hat on, slip into the vest, and I'll be set to go. If you need help zipping up your dress, I--"

"I won't need any help whatsoever!" I say, cutting him off before he can finish that thought, shuffling into the bathroom and slamming the door behind me.

"Wait, where's the lock?" I shout through the door.

"What'd'ya need a lock for? I'm not barging in the bathroom on you. Hurry up and change, Grace! We need to get going!"

"I don't even know where we're going, Dare!"

"To the parade, woman! Didn't I say that before?"

"I don't see why I..." And the rest of my words are a grumble of nothingness as I begrudgingly slip out of my perfectly fine clothes and into this... this crazy green, off-the-shoulder ball gown.

It's actually pretty easy to get into. Without sleeves to speak of, and just some slightly immodest, lace satin shoulder straps, I pretty much slip into it and that's it.

Except the zipper in the back. Why is it always the zipper in the back? I tug it up halfway, but for the life of me I can't get it the rest of the way up. I usually only wear dresses for plays, and when you're in a dressing room backstage you have more than enough people who can help you with a zipper or two now and then.

Right now? I have Dare Mackenzie and I wouldn't trust him with a zipper if my life depended on it. More than likely it'll end up down rather than up, and I didn't wear the right set of bra and panties for a situation like that.

If I'm about to get seduced, I'd have at least liked to have come in a nice lacy black set of underwear instead of--

I, um... I didn't just think that. I mean, it's true, but I refuse to accept that I totally just thought that. We're going to strike that from the records, thank you very much.

"You need help with that zipper yet?" Dare asks, standing outside the bathroom door.

"...I do," I admit, reluctant. "But I want it to go up, not down!"

"Shite, which way's up again?" he asks. "You want me to make it closer to the ground, yeah?"

"The sky!" I shout through the door. "Up is to the sky, Dare Mackenzie!"

"Aye, like the color of your eyes." He laughs and wiggles the doorknob. "Can I open her up?"

Ugh. The way he says that. Can I open her up? Like he's asking if he can... open up other things...

With my legs spread, his face inches away from my arousal-slick folds, glistening with anticipation as his warm, soft breath teases across my sensual, blossoming flower.

Yes, that was all very poetic and nice, but that's just what I thought of immediately after he asked if he could open her up.

And, yes, I *know* he means the door. This isn't my fault, dammit. It's my bad girl tendencies. They're sneaking in when they shouldn't. I don't even know where they came from! I used to have good girl tendencies, and now I have bad girl ones.

I can't even believe this. Ugh. I sneak away for one weekend and then this happens.

"Yes," I say, trying to hide every single thought I just had.

The door sneaks open and Dare peeks in. Once he sees I'm dressed with my back turned to him, he pulls the door open all the way. One hand slides down the bare skin of my back to the zipper, while the other tugs lightly at the fabric up top. The zipper slides up easily, settling in nicely at the top.

Dare reaches for my hand, wraps his fingers in mine, and spins me around to take a look at me.

"My God," he says, smiling bright. "Grace Turner, if you're not the most beautiful girl I've ever laid eyes on..."

"Shush!" I say, playfully slapping at his cheeks with the tips of my fingers. "This is a nice vest. Is it yours?"

I pull at the vest, my fingers slipping close to the buttons holding it closed.

"Aye. You like it?"

"Don't get any ideas, lover boy," I remind him. "You said we're going to the parade, and you got me into this crazy green dress so I expect something really great now."

"Greater than great, Grace Turner," he says, teasing his fingers across my cheekbone quickly. "You'll never forget it."

DARE

W ell, not sure what's gotten into me, but I find myself not wanting to disappoint the amazingly beautiful Grace Turner. And that she is. Amazingly beautiful, that is. She wears the green gown like she was born to it, like a princess in a fairytale who's finally discovered her true self.

Not that Grace needed any discovering for that to happen. I imagine she's known her true self for awhile now, might be she's always known it, but for whatever reason she's rippin' to do something out of the ordinary, so...

I like a challenge and this seems like a fun way to pass St. Paddy's Day if I do say so myself. Let's get to it, Turner.

That's my cue to drag her all through the streets of Dublin, winding this way and that, her dress roaring up with the wind as she attempts to tame the glorious green fabric. She runs in her sneakers; a clash of fashion right there. But despite her best intentions the dress holds her back.

"Why am I in this dress again?" she asks as we take one final turn.

"You'll see," I tell her, grinning wide.

She smiles back at me, a smile as bright as the sun on a clear summer day overlooking the Cliffs of Moher.

"Are you always this much trouble?" she insinuates.

"Aye, at least this much," I admit, then with a wry smirk I add, "Catch me on a good day and you'll see the sorts of mischief I can get into."

"What? This isn't a good day? I would've thought it's your best considering you've met me."

"Oh! My American girl with feisty jokes and an ego, eh? 'Tis true, though. Can't think of a better day than this, which is likely why I'm pulling out all the stops. Are you impressed yet, Grace?"

"Impressed by--"

But we're here and I don't have time to answer her. There's not much time for it as the parade's starting any minute. I step forward, confronting the pair standing atop the wooden parade float. They stare down at me with wicked grins plastered across their faces.

"Oi! Dermot! Shannon! I've met an American girl!" I shout up to them even if they're only a couple meters away.

"What?" Dermot asks, glancing this way and that. "An American girl? Where?"

"Right here," I say, spinning on the balls of my feet and

gesturing to Grace with a ringmaster's flourish. "A stunner, eh?"

"Stop mocking the poor American girl, Dare!" Shannon bellows at me, hands propped on her hips, flouncy dress bouncing as she admonishes me.

"'S'not mocking if it's true, innit?" I counter.

Grace blushes and mumbles, staring at the toes of her sneakers. Never really thought it before now, but I'm sure she has beautiful toes, too. Just like the rest of her. Do you think toes can be beautiful? I'm sure Grace's are. Beauty from head to toes, so they have to be, yeah?

Dermot takes a moment to admire my American girl. Good on him, that's the only thing he'll get from her. He knows it, too. I give him that look mates give each other. Sorry, Dermot, but she's mine. If she'll have me, that is. But I won't give up easily, Grace. That's a promise.

Shannon's a bit more circumspect. She shakes her head, knowing full well what I'm up to. And what of it, Shannon? Can't I seduce a beautiful American girl now and then? Or just the once. Once is all I need, honestly. Because...

Well, we'll talk about that later at the pub, yeah?

"Anyways, what's it you want, Dare Mackenzie?" Shannon asks, accusation for an entire century's worth of wrongdoing dripping in her voice.

"She wants to see the parade. Mind if we swap?"

"I have a name!" Grace interrupts.

"She's got a name, by the way," I tell them. "A good one! Grace Turner. Soon to be Mackenzie. I'm making her mine."

"You are not!" Grace says, giving me that same hands-on-hips look Shannon's already giving me.

Two at once. That's a feat.

"She's feisty," I point out.

"Why should we let you up on this float?" Shannon asks, ignoring my playful banter with Grace to get down to high business. "I've spent months preparing for this."

"I only spent a day," Dermot adds. "Didn't seem too hard."

"Shut your mouth, Dermot!" Shannon says, pointing a finger at him. "I'll tell your ma what an arse you are if you don't."

"You think she doesn't know what an arse I am already?" he asks, lifting a brow at her.

"I'll tell her something even worse!"

They bicker back and forth for awhile, as they do. I wait it out while Grace fidgets side to side. Aye, not so much of a bad girl now, are ya? Not that I ever thought she was in truth, nor did I ever want her to be. We are what we are and that's the best part of being yourself if you ask me.

"I'll make you a deal," I tell the two of them on the float once they settle down after riling each other up. "You switch places with me and I'll let you hear Grace's terrible Irish accent at the pub later."

"Hey! I do not have a terrible Irish accent!" Grace says, slapping at my shoulder.

"Sounds like an American accent to me," Dermot says with a nod.

"Should've heard her earlier. When we first met, she tried to get me to shove off by acting like she was Irish."

"Is that all it takes to get you to shove off?" Shannon asks. "Wish I'd known earlier. I'd have acted even more Irish around you this entire time."

"Oi, Shannon, come now, you couldn't live without me."

"I think I could! 'Specially if you're loaning my dresses to random American girls, even if she looks absolutely gorgeous in it," she says, sneaking a wink to Grace with the last part.

"Oh, is this your dress?" Grace asks, tugging at the skirt. "It's very pretty. Thank--"

"Should've heard her cursing it out while we were running here," I spout off. Mocking, adding a bit of high pitch to my voice, I say, "*Why* am I in this dress again, *Dare Macken-zie? Ugh!*"

"I didn't say it like that!" Grace says, laughing and pushing my shoulder again.

"I think we should let them swap, Shannon," Dermot says to his lovely girlfriend.

"You think?" Shannon says, smirking back at him. "It's never going to work. I can already tell."

"I'm a-hundred percent sure I can do it!" I announce to the entire world, which at the moment is only the four of us and a few people from nearby floats who are staring after us.

"I've already put the dress on and my clothes are back at... I think, your place?" Grace says to Shannon. "I didn't really know what I was getting into, and I don't want to steal your float away from you."

"Nah, this float's a huge hassle," Shannon says, hopping down from the float. "Dermot, help the American girl up!

Dare, you climb up on your own. Go. Shoo! Get on with it. You've told her what this is about, yeah?"

"Not even a little!" I say, a wicked grin fast upon my lips.

I climb up the side of the float and hold out my hand to help Grace up before Dermot's even got a shot at it. He grunts and shakes his head at me, acting discouraged.

"Won't even let me touch her hand, eh? This must be serious, mate. Don't you two go falling in love or anything."

"Like that would ever happen!" Grace shouts at me.

Oi, I'm not the one who said it, love. Don't blame me for this.

"She's already in love with me, she's just playing hard to get," I say to my friend with a wink and a nod.

Can blame me for that one, though.

"Have fun, you two!" Shannon says, waving at us. "Dermot, let's go find a spot near the end so we can see just how awfully Dare fails at this."

"That's a bit harsh, Shannon," he says, taking her hand in his. "If he fails that bad we're going to have to buy him rounds after so he can drink away his sorrows, and then one of us is going to have to drag him back to his flat when he's drunk."

"True," she says, thoughtful. "Well, we all know you're gonna fail, Dare. But don't fail so bad that you're heartbroken and crying in your Guinness. That's not the St. Paddy's Day way, you hear?"

"Oh ye of little faith," I say, standing tall. "Get yourselves to church or something. Don't need none of your faithlessness on this most glorious of days."

34

"You haven't even told her, Dare Mackenzie! Might be I'd have a bit more faith if you'd of told her, but as is stands--"

"Um, what exactly do I need to be told?" Grace asks.

"I'm gonna tell her right now," I say, shaking a fist at my friends. Turning to Grace, I say, "I'm gonna tell you, beautiful, but you have to promise not to get mad, alright?"

I imagine you're not supposed to say those words to someone you've just met, but it is what it is. Also, her cheeks turn a lovely shade of angry red as she glowers at me, eyebrows knit up with a bit of rage. Just a bit. It's cute. Reminds me of the way my mum looked at my dad right before they stormed off saying they needed to have a private discussion in the bedroom.

Right. Of course.

It's a miracle I don't have twenty brothers and sisters if you ask me.

GRACE

"**E**xcuse me?" I say, mad before he's even started telling me anything. "Why should I promise not to get mad at you? What are you pulling me into, Dare Mackenzie?"

And I give him *that* look. *Definitely* one of *those* looks. The look that all men cower in fear over, except Dare's not just any ordinary man. A smile splits his face and he cracks into laughter while I give him an evil, ominous glare of doom.

"Aww, don't get upset, Princess."

"Um, did you just call me Princess?" I ask, because this seems like it needs asking.

"Aye, you're dressed up like one, yeah? You're a Celtic Princess for the parade, Grace. Need to put on a bit of the ol' poise and grace and stand tall with a right regal look about you. Thought you said you were some fancy actress back in the States?"

"I mean, I'm in the drama club and I act in plays, but they're just for school," I mumble, suddenly aware of exactly what I'm wearing and where I am.

It's not like the dress is bad or anything. Altogether it's very flattering and nice. But... I'm standing atop a parade float that's about to circle through the streets of Dublin and I'm dressed in a posh ball gown as green as a four-leaf clover, with "Celtic Princess" as my *modus operandi* of the hour.

"Maybe a bow and arrow'll help?" Dare offers. "Pretend your mum's a bear?"

"Excuse me!" I protest, trying hard not to laugh. "Merida was *Scottish*. That's not even Celtic, that's Gaelic. Her dress looks nothing like mine and I don't have red curly hair, so..."

"Oh, you're a keeper, Grace Turner. Knowing the difference between Scottish and Irish, Celtic and Gaelic. Aye, I'll definitely keep you around. If you're staying, that is. Tell me you'll stay with me forever, or at least until the end of the day."

He tops that last part off with an exaggerated wink and a silly grin.

Ugh. I hate how handsome he is when he's teasing me. It's like everything's a silly joke, but he also means every words he says.

You can just kiss my bare arse, Dare! Yeah, that's right! I can use, um... Irish words... I mean, arse isn't that much of an Irish thing, I don't think, but it made me feel better for half a second.

Also, no, you *can't* kiss my bare arse. You'd like it to

much. Which is why I say none of this to him. I'll never hear the end of it.

"You haven't even told me what we're doing," I politely inform him, perfectly princess-like. "I can't stay the day with you if you aren't open and honest with me, now can I?"

"Hmm, that's something, innit?" he asks, tapping his index finger to his lips. "True, true. Well, what we're supposed to play at atop this grande ol float is that you're the Celtic Princess and I'm the tricky leprechaun. I've got promises of gold and wonder for you, but I'll only ever trade my wisdom for a kiss."

"Which you're never going to get," I inform him, again very politely, arms crossed over my chest, regal as can be.

"There ya go! That's the spirit," he says, nodding twice. "Just keep it up until the end and then I'll swoop in for that kiss, yeah?"

"I thought you said I should do my best to fight you off," I counter. "Meaning, I'm never going to kiss you, Dare Mackenzie. Not in a million years. Especially not today. We've only just met. I don't know what you think as far as American girls go, but I'm nothing like it."

"I'd never dare dream you were," he says, all of a sudden sweet and genuine, eyes sparkling green like sunlight shining through a forest canopy. "I'll still be doing my best to get you to let me kiss you, Grace Turner. If not today, I can assure you I'll keep trying the next day, and the day after that, and--"

His words trail off as his sweetness turns a little silly. And I like it. I like what he's saying and what he's doing, and if I'm honest and open with myself I wouldn't mind kissing him right here and not, just... not on top of a float in the middle of the St. Paddy's Day parade in Dublin.

It does seem kind of romantic, though. I just...

If not today, I don't think it'll be ever, because I'm leaving tomorrow. And I know the entire point of coming to Dublin for the weekend was to let loose, be a little wild, have at it with some of those naughty bad girl tendencies I've always wanted act out, but as far as this goes, I just don't think I can do it.

A part of me wants to. More than a little part, too. Dare's fun and adventurous and unlike anyone I've ever met before. The way he looks at me is both part depraved naughtiness and another part sweet puppy dog eyes. It's like he wants to do terrible dirty things to me and then cuddle with me while we look up at the stars.

The problem is that I know if I have a taste, even one little ounce of the snack that is Dare Mackenzie, I'll want more. And more is completely off the table. We're an entire ocean apart except for this one single day of luck and fate.

"Penny for your thoughts?" Dare asks, sliding up beside me and wrapping his arm about my waist.

"Is this your attempt at sneaking in close for a kiss?" I ask, turning up my nose at him.

"Can't blame me for trying?" he asks, his fingers wrapping tight around my hip and squeezing slightly.

"I can blame you for a whole lot of things if I want to," I say, looking away, giving him absolutely no access to my lips.

"You're so beautiful, Grace," Dare says. "You're smart and feisty and your hair looks like sunshine and I bet your lips taste like strawberries. Do you mind if I admit I'm going to enjoy trying to kiss you? Even if it's not to be and our paths were never meant to cross so close, I'm happy I met you."

I blush, turning back to him slightly, but not enough to make him think I fully approve of his flattery. Because I don't. Except I do. And I love how he said that, the whole 'even if our paths were never meant to cross so close' thing. It's poetic and beautiful, but he's saying it about me which makes me feel like a beautiful poem all on my own.

"You're starting off very strong," I tell him, hoping to keep my tone steady. "Maybe you should save some of that charm for the rest of the parade, lover boy."

"Haven't started at all yet," he says, flashing a quick grin my way. "Wanted you to know the truth, Grace Turner. It's how I've felt from the moment we met and the feelings're growing stronger every moment I spend with you. I'll start trying to kiss you in earnest once we're on our way, which should be--"

"Are ya ready up there!" a man shouts from below, waving his arm roughly in our direction.

"Aye, we are!" Dare shouts back, slipping away from me and taking his place on the opposite side of the float. With a gentle wink to me, he adds, "If you can't keep your lips to yourself, I won't be complaining. Not much, at least."

"Oh, they're staying to themselves," I say, shaking my head at him before tossing my hair over my shoulder. "Hope you won't mind missing the sweet taste of strawberries."

"If I only ever tasted them when my lips touched yours,

I'd miss them every single day of my life waiting for you, love."

I can't even.

Seriously, with Dare Mackenzie I have completely lost my ability to "even."

It is gone. Erased from existence.

Ugh.

I love everything he says, which is how I know he's the most dangerous man in the world.

I did come here wanting to be a bad girl though, didn't I?

Maybe I've found my true calling...

DARE

I'm a man on a mission at the moment. Not a mission to kiss my beautiful American girl, though. Nah, we've all the time in the world for that. Isn't fun if she doesn't desperately want to kiss me back, either. We're working up to it, Grace and I, and a bit of anticipation is more than half the fun, yeah?

The mission's more about making sure we do a right proper job of this parade, plus I need to show her the city while we go, and then there's the acting to take care of.

I might've lured the beautiful Grace Turner here under mysterious circumstances but now that we're into it we've work to do!

Look, it's not like my job's hard. I'll be spending the next hour teasing and tormenting her trying to get her to kiss me while sneaking in whispers about this or that or whatever else other delightful things I decide to whisper in her ear.

Sounds like a proper good time if you ask me.

"Kiss me," I say to her, loud, for all the crowd to hear.

"Never," she says, headstrong and sturdy.

Oh, the things you do to me, Grace. Never have I ever been so turned on by a girl denying me a kiss.

"If you kiss me, I'll give you everything you've ever wanted," I tell her, working in a few leprechaun tricks. Not that I've ever met one in person, but I think we all know how that goes.

"If you give me everything I want, there won't be any satisfaction in it," she says, shaking her head. "The fun comes in achieving things for yourself, not in having them handed to you for free without any effort."

"Oh, I can think of a lot of *effort* and *achievement* we can get up to if you'll lay your lips on mine, beautiful. Plenty o' satisfaction in it for ya, too."

"Dare!" Grace says, giggling like a madwoman. "There's... there's, um..." She glances to the side at a handful of children watching us, who are also laughing. Whispering, she adds, "There's kids! Be good!"

"Kiss me and I won't say anything else inappropriate for the entire day," I say, crossing my heart with two fingers. "Don't want to ruin your poor prude sensibilities seeing as you're American and all."

"Kiss him!" one of the laughing kids shouts out. This starts a full on chant from the whole lot of 'em. Over and over. "Kiss him, kiss him, kiss him!"

Sneaking in close, acting like I'm going for a kiss whether she wants one or not, I whisper to her, "It's only silly banter, beautiful. No one'll think anything of it and I'll keep it tame enough for the kids."

"I... I guess so," she mumbles, sticking her tongue out at me.

"Now slap me like I've offended you, but don't go all crazy on me now. Let's give 'em a good show, yeah?"

She smirks, then winds back her hand and smacks me across the cheek. Oi, she's good. She pulls her punch, or her smack if you will, and what looks like a harsh pounding ends in barely more than a playful caress.

Grace Turner can caress my cheek any day of the week, even if it's a bank holiday, even if she's acting like she's slapping me to the moon and back.

"She's a stubborn lass, that's for sure," I say, spinning around like a top. I glance out over the crowd, looking for help hither or yon. "Anyone got any ideas?"

"You can't get ideas from them!" Grace protests, standing at my side. Giving the crowd a stern talking to, she says, "Don't tell him anything!"

Like good old Irish boys and girls, men and women, old and young, they all start shouting out tricks for me to try in getting my lovely Celtic Princess to give in to my charm.

"Tickle her!" someone says.

"What!" Grace says right back, acting shocked. She's a beauty, alright. Everyone starts to laugh.

I reach over like I'm about to tickle her side but she just slaps my hand away and wags her finger at me.

"Kiss him first!" a little girl shouts to Grace. "Then he will nae be able to kiss ya. He'll be stunned!"

"Hm, kiss him first?" Grace says, peeking over at me.

I pucker up my lips and blink one eye closed.

"No~pe!" she says, smirking at me.

"What about me! Give me ideas, not her!" I shout out.

"Tell her a joke," someone suggests.

"Marry her," another adds.

"Is *that* the joke?" I ask.

"I'll marry you as soon as I kiss you, which is to say, *never*," Grace says, putting on a pouty face and turning her back to me.

"Tell her she's pretty!" a wee little lass says, bright eyes beaming up at me.

"Aye, I'll try that," I say, winking at the girl. "Grace Turner, you're the prettiest woman I've ever laid eyes on. You're prettier than a rainbow with a pot o' gold at the end."

"I bet you say that about all the rainbows," Grace says, shaking her head.

"I'd give up every rainbow and all my gold if I could get one little taste of your lips."

"Then what kind of leprechaun would you be?" she asks.

"I'd give that up, too. I'll be an honest man for you, Grace Turner. I'll get a job working at the docks."

"But what if something happens to you?" she asks, playing along. "If we fall in love and you get a job at the docks and you fall into the water, and... heaven forbid it, but..."

"I'll learn to swim right then and there, immediate, on the spot! And I'll bring you a family of otters, too. They'll be cute as can be and they'll adore you."

"Now you're just mocking me," she says, hands right back

on her hips as she glowers my way.

"I'll bring you every four-leaf clover that's ever existed!"

"Five," she counters. "I want a five-leaf clover."

"Did ya hear that?" I ask the crowd. "So demanding. I've almost got her, though. She's right where I want her."

"I seem to still be standing, with all my clothes on, and not a bed in sight, so I hardly think I'm *right* where you want me, Dare Mackenzie."

And at that, the crowd goes wild. Oi. It's true, too. If I had my pick of having Grace anywhere I wanted, I'm not sure this'd be it. In bed'd be nice, though. After a few pints at the pub and a night of lively music and even livelier conversation.

Aye, Grace Turner, I might have to take you up on that later. If we get that far. I don't want to wind up doing anything you'd regret. I'd regret it even more if we did.

But if we're not regretting anything, well...

A kiss on the lips will never be enough. I want to kiss every single millimeter of your body, Grace. I want to know exactly how you taste in every sense of the word, every part of your being, every piece of your soul.

That's the God's honest truth. None of this acting or playing for a crowd. But I know I can't tell you that, either. It's not fair, would never be fair.

We'll be an ocean apart soon enough, and as much as I like swimming, I don't think it's fair to ask you to wait for me that long.

If she wants to wait on her own, though...

I swim fast. Promise.

GRACE

The silly banter goes back and forth between us. I'm running out of reasons not to kiss Dare, too. I know this is an act, we're playing for a crowd, but if I was playing for myself, well... I'd wrap my arms around him and tell him he should really just kiss me now.

Some of it has to do with the way he is with everyone around us. He's loud and boisterous, but in the most kind and considerate way. He listens to the little ones as they stumble on words trying to tell him their plans. And he smiles at the elderly as they stand and wink at him, looking between the two of us like we must already be lovers.

This is completely not my naughty side talking, but... I could absolutely see myself being his lover, too. Not in a casual way. I get the feeling that despite all of his attempts to persuade me otherwise, Dare Mackenzie is anything but casual.

Intense, fierce, intelligent, with a body made for sin, and a mouth made for worse, like confessing his love with every breath he takes, Dare is the kind of bad boy who would sweep me off my feet, take me to meet his parents, and then afterwards never let me leave his bed if I didn't have a good reason to.

I'm almost out of reasons why we shouldn't do that, either.

"We're coming up on the Guinness Storehouse," Dare whispers, covertly pointing towards the building with a tell-tale harp on a sign outside. "Good for a tour and a pint, but you can get stout just as fresh in all the good pubs throughout Dublin."

In between our silly fun he's been showing me the sights of the Irish city. We've gone by Dublin castle, this beautiful medieval Viking history centre, even more beautiful build-ings than I can count, and one or two whiskey distilleries. It's all amazing and more wonderful than I ever could have imagined.

"I'd've loved to have shown you the zoo," he adds, another whisper under his breath while we take a break from the crowd. "Or a train ride over to Galway to see the other side of Ireland. It's a beautiful country, Grace. I hope you're enjoying our small piece of it right here."

"You make it easy to enjoy," I whisper, smiling at him.

"Yeah?" he asks, grinning wide.

And then, for whatever reason, I'm not even sure why myself, I say, "I never get to play fun roles. All the comedy ones are taken by other girls because they say I'm too serious or that no one will take me seriously if I play a funny role. I really like this, Dare. I like being silly with you. I..."

I trail off before I can say something that I can't take back. I want to, but I know that if I say it that it might be too much.

"I'm glad you're having fun," he says, teasing his hand up along my hip, intimate and close. "I'd put you in every role I could if it was me making the choice. You're beautiful, you're smart, you're a riot and you've made everyone laugh out loud more than not, and you're an absolute joy, Grace. The only thing I think's a little too serious about you is that I seriously would love to press my lips against yours. You're the most kissable woman I've ever laid eyes on. Whole truth, Grace Turner. Not a tease or a lie or anything besides. The parade's nearly done and as much as I've had fun being with you I'm not acting anymore."

"Oh?" I ask, teasing him, lifting one brow, coy. "Would you like to kiss me? Actually?"

"Aye, I would," he says. "Just once, though."

"Not twice?"

"If I kissed you twice I'd fall in love and never be able to kiss any other girl ever again."

He smirks, trying to play it off, but the look in his eye is the most serious and vulnerable I've ever seen. This is open intimacy on a level I never dreamed existed, and I'm not sure I can handle it. I can't handle it because...

"I like you," I tell him, leaning close, our lips nearly touching. And then I pull back, grinning and giggling but my eyes never leave his. "Kiss me, Dare Mackenzie. I want you to kiss me. Not as a leprechaun, not as part of the parade, but as yourself. Like you mean it."

He takes my hand in his and spins me about like when we first met. I move with him easily, the easiest thing in the entire world.

"Aye?" he asks. "Are you sure that's enough?"

His hand cradles my back and he dips me low, his mouth scandalously close to mine.

I reach up and cup his cheeks in my hands, gently rubbing my thumbs down to the corner of his lips.

"Please?" I say.

Slow, like time stopped and we've got the rest of eternity to make this perfect, he leans closer and kisses me. As soon as our lips touch, time bursts back to life. The crowd around us, having watched the banter and seeing me telling Dare that I'd never kiss him, not in a million years, roars victoriously, celebrating my trickster leprechaun's success.

I kiss him back, soft, taking my time. Our lips enjoy each other, exploring, teasing, tasting.

This is only one kiss, right? It just lasts for a really long time...

DARE

"Well, this is it, Grace Turner," I tell her, holding my hand out to help her climb down from the float in her fancy flouncy dress. "I hope you've had a grande time but I've got to be on my way now."

"What?" she asks, staring at me like I've just slapped her hard across the face.

I get it. I really do. But between the two of us there'll be more than enough heartbreak to last a lifetime if we keep this up. Aye, I knew what I was getting myself into, but that doesn't mean I should keep digging deeper, now does it?

"I may have been playing as a leprechaun, but a Mackenzie never lies," I say, swallowing hard, determined to do this the proper, gentlemanly way. "I meant it, Grace. If I invite you to the pub with me I'm going to want to kiss you again before the night's through. And if I kiss you again I'll fall madly in love with you for the rest of my life."

That's just the way it is, my American girl. I'm hopeless like that. Can't help it. They say Ireland's a land of literature and poets, and maybe some of us don't fall in love as easily as that, but that's only because we haven't met the one we're supposed to fall in love with.

When you meet her, though... aye, you'll know it.

I've tried telling myself otherwise this past hour, but it's not working out so well for me. I need to break it off before my American girl and I hurt ourselves something fierce. A broken heart's the worst kind of pain.

I'm sure Grace knows it, too. Aye, she'll admit it any second now. She's a good girl, she is. She'll have a beautiful time the rest of the day, go on back to America where she belongs, and find someone who--

"What?" she asks, opening her mouth, shock and sass full on circling her lips like the most beautiful shade of lipstick God's ever created. "You're not in love with me already? The nerve of you, Dare Mackenzie!"

Nevermind. I take it all back. There's nothing good about Grace Turner. She's the worst kind of awful, the type that you can't seem to ever get rid of even when you know you should. She's that cat that knocks all your priceless glass trinkets off the counter, and then she stares up at you with sweetness in her eyes wanting you to pet her kindly.

Never could turn down a cat who wants a scritch or two behind the ears.

What I'm saying is that Grace Turner has nine lives and

altogether she wants me to ruin each and every one of them in the most absolute naughtiest way possible, all while the good girl part of her looks at me with sweetness and smiles and tender affection.

You think you can handle that, my lovely American girl?

We'll see.

I shake my head, testing and teasing her. "You're welcome to follow me to the pub. I'll introduce you to my mates properly this time. You met the two earlier but there's more where that came from. You've been warned, though. Take it as you will."

"I do appreciate the warning," she says, subtly sly, slinking close to me like sensual sin. "And I wouldn't want to ruin your life by making you fall in love with me, so..."

"Don't go thinking I'll kiss you again that easy," I say, smirking hard at her.

It would be that easy, though. If she doesn't move away I'll make her mine right here and now. Fuck the parade. I'll drag her into the nearest broom closet if I have to, and then I'll spend a lifetime with her making up for how unromantic my first romantic gesture was. I can think of worse ways to live.

She skips away, but not before reaching out to tangle her fingers in mine. We hold hands like that, or at least we hold fingers for a time, but like all the best things in the world it doesn't last forever.

"We should head back and change into regular clothes. Then you'll be much less tempted to kiss me. I won't have as much cleavage for you to stare at, for one. And I won't keep imagining you as a leprechaun coming in to steal a kiss from me, either. That should work to cool us down, right?"

"Aye, you think that's enough to cool me down?" I ask.

I take a few long moments to admire her fine cleavage on full display. Dresses like that do wonders for the age old pastime of staring at a beautiful girl's breasts.

"Dare Mackenzie! Are you staring at my breasts?" she asks, playfully offended, holding her hands up to cover herself for whatever good that does.

"Kiss me now and I'll do hell of a lot more than stare at them," I say, growling at her.

"Will you now?" she asks, tucking her bottom lip between her teeth. "Like what?"

"You're damned lucky it's a holiday today or else I'd drag you to the nearest church, shout for all I'm worth until a priest came out asking what's with the riot, and I'd beg him to marry us on the spot so I could drag you off and consummate our wedding in every position possible. That's what."

"I... what... um..." She gapes at me like I'm a wizard straight out of a Harry Potter book and I've just mesmerized her with a confundus charm.

Aye, well, stop being so damned bewitching, Grace Turner. Or should I call her Grace Mackenzie now and be done with it? I'm committed.

"You heard me," I say, grinning wide at her. "Would you like me to repeat myself, though?"

"I... I don't think I we can get married yet because you'd have to ask for my father's permission," she says, dumb-founded.

I laugh, booming. Oi. It's true, too. I'd want to do that.

I stuff my hand into my pocket and pull out my phone. "What's his number?" I ask, casual, ready to dial.

"Dare! You can't call my dad right now!"

"What? Why not? You said I need his permission. Let's do this proper, yeah?"

"Um, he's not going to give it to you! Also, he... he doesn't know I'm here?"

"American girl," I say, because I'm rather fond of calling her it at this point. Don't judge me. "You mean to tell me you've come all the way across an ocean. Maybe all the way across the States, as well. And you never told your parents?"

"When you say it like that it sounds worse than it is," she says.

"You're wild," I tell her, shaking my head.

"That's the whole point!" she says, pouting at me. "Everyone expects me to be some perfect good girl all the time and I don't get to have fun and I know that studying and practicing volleyball and performing in plays, and doing the responsible thing is a good idea for the future, but it doesn't exactly leave me a lot of time for myself, you know?"

"Volleyball, eh?" I ask, lifting both eyebrows. "Don't suppose you brought those short shorts with you, did ya?"

My American girl is so damned sexy when she puts her hands on her hips and glares at me like that. Shite. I'm screwed, I am.

"No, I did *not*," she says, harnessing her inner Irish fury on this fine St. Paddy's Day afternoon. "Not that I'd ever wear them just so you could ogle my butt, either!"

"So you're saying you'll take them off before letting me stare at your arse?" I ask.

"You're naughty," she says, hands even firmer on her hips.

"You want to be naughty with me?" I ask her.

"Yes," she says, grinning bright. "But I'm not going to! You'd fall in love with me and then you'd just end up following me around like a puppy dog and I'd feel bad."

"Aye, we can't have that, now can we?" I say, shaking my head. "I can already tell you're in love with me, so I'm holding back something fierce. If I actually tried, we'd never get to the pub and my mates would be upset at you for ruining the rounds of Guinness we'll soon be ordering. Considering you're going to be my wife once I figure out your father's phone number, I think we should start this off a little slower and not get straight to the naughty bits."

"You act like I'm the only one who wants to do anything naughty," she says, pouting at me. "I don't like that. It's not fair."

"Grace Turner, since I met you hardly a second's gone by that I didn't want to do something naughty with you. You give me far too much credit, woman."

Aye, there she goes. That's the blush I wanted to see. Red like a Rosette apple and liable to be just as sweet. I'd kiss it off her cheek for a taste but then I'd never be able to keep my lips off of her.

Patience, lad.

GRACE

"Hey! You haven't murdered him yet!" Shannon shouts out to me through the small pub when Dare and I walk in. "Can I get you a drink? We're doing rounds."

Yes, Dare's a handful. I may have also been incredibly tempted to let him have more than a handful while we were back at Shannon's apartment changing into our regular clothes. I slipped into the tiny bathroom again to undress, and my emerging bad girl tendencies told me it would be a stellar idea to also slip out of the bathroom while completely undressed.

The look on Dare's face would have been worth it. And then what?

I mean... what if I sashayed across the room, took his hand in mine, and laid it on my chest, his palm cupping one breast, feeling his heat, both his hand and his heated stare on my bare body.

Mhm. Definitely more than a handful, Dare Mackenzie. Do you think you can handle me?

You wouldn't have believed I could do that even if you tried.

He does have big hands so maybe not that much more than a handful, but at that point I don't think either of us would be counting or keeping track.

And, I did *not* do that, but I worked myself up plenty imagining it. Damn you, Dare Mackenzie! What are you doing to me?

"What can I get ya?" a girl in server's gear asks, coming up to the table once I'm about to sit down.

"A pint of Guinness?" I ask.

"Aye, that's the way!" Shannon says, cheering me on. "Here, sit next to me. Dare, you go on and sit over there. You've had plenty of time with the American girl. Leave some fun for the rest of us."

"Don't go stealing my wife, Shannon!" Dare says, winking at her.

"Wife! Gosh. Someone tie Dare up. He's in too deep. Is that why you haven't murdered him yet, Grace? What's he been whispering to you?"

I mumble a few words, unsure what to say. It also doesn't help that the waitress seems a little overly friendly with the guy who just declared me his wife. Does he do this often, or...?

"Pint of Guinness for me too, love," he says to the girl. "Anyone else? I'll get the next round."

Everyone at the table takes up their glasses and swallows down what's left, and the orders go through, a full round for the lot of us. I can't even imagine doing anything like this with the girls back home on my volleyball squad. They'd die of embarrassment.

I'm pretty close to it myself! Um...

"Jus' teasing ya, by the way," Shannon says, sneaking in close so we can have as much of a private conversation as is possible in the corner of a crowded Irish bar on St. Patrick's Day. "Dare's a good guy. Aye, he likes to talk big, but he's not as bad as he makes out."

"Except for that time he nearly jumped into the river to escape Margaret," Dermot adds.

"What? Are we telling all my most embarrassing stories?" Dare asks. "Look, Margaret's tried to get her hooks into me since grade school and if I have to swim across a river now and then to save myself, dammit I'll do it."

I laugh and shake my head. "What did Margaret ever do to you?" I ask, teasing him.

"Oi, Grace, she tried to make me chocolates all the time. Brought over tupperware full of stew or bangers and mash, which she well knows are my favorites. Tried giving me a pup once. Wee little pup, cute as can be. Said her beagle'd snuck out and got knocked up and if I'd want a pup this was the best one."

"How terrible," I say, rolling my eyes.

"Don't worry. She's long done now. This was ages ago.

Margaret's found a good man who adores her bangers and mash."

"I'd say adores banging her considering they've got three kids now too," Shannon pipes in.

"Shannon! Don't corrupt my pure American girl's sensibilities with words like that," Dare says, winking at me.

"Don't make me tell them what you were saying to me earlier..." I say. Two can play at this game, Dare Mackenzie!

"Yeah? What was good ol' Dare saying now?" Shannon asks, ears perked up. "Are we gonna have to start some foreign relations here? Get the American ambassador involved?"

"Think Grace and I can do well enough with our *foreign relations* without involving an American ambassador," Dare says to her, then to me he adds, "Right, beautiful?"

"If we *must*..." I say, letting out a playful sigh. "I mean, you're already in love with me, so..."

"Not yet," he says. "Kiss me again and we'll see, though."

"Again?!" Shannon shrieks, both excited and annoyed. "What? When did this happen? Do I need to clean my sheets?"

"Come on now," Dermot says, shaking his head. "Not Shannon's poor sheets, you two."

"Nothing inappropriate happened on the bed!" I say, laughing.

"The couch?" one of Dare's other friends offers.

"Who says it's got to be laying down?" the girl on the opposite side of Shannon adds. "Might be they cleaned up real nice in the shower."

"Can't do nothin' in that shower, let me tell you," Shannon says, narrowing her eyes, perturbed. "If Dermot and I can't manage it, these two who are five times as tall if they're a centimeter couldn't do it. It's a good place, don't get me wrong. I love my flat for all it's worth, but for getting dirty in the shower it's not worth a whole lot. Don't even get me started."

"Think you've gotten yourself plenty started already, love," Dermot says to her, smirking.

"Don't you even get me started more, Dermot!" Shannon says, shaking a fist at him.

The serving girl comes back with our pints right then, handing them out to us. I look into the deep, dark stout, excited. Not just for another taste of this forbidden drink, the type of thing I could never be seen with back home, but because this St. Patrick's Day is more than I ever could have imagined.

"What's that beautiful smile on your lips all about, Grace Turner?" Dare asks, leaning across the table and smiling at me.

"Today's been a lot of fun," I tell him, truthful.

"Cheers to that," he says, hoisting up his glass.

"Aye! Let's let our lovely new American friend do the first cheers," Shannon says, holding up her glass.

"You're stealing it from her!" Dermot says, teasing her.

I hold up my pint of Guinness. "Cheers to a really fun St. Paddy's Day!" I say.

Clink.

Clink clink clink clink clink.

DARE

onight's looking like a rowdy one for my favorite pub. It's a bit on the smaller side, but I like her. Me and my mates come here at least once or twice a week to wind down and enjoy our friendship and the company of others. There's the usuals who're always here, but on a day like St. Paddy's Day you get those one or two out-of-towners who are looking for that real Ireland experience.

Truth be told, you can get it just about anywhere if you're looking. Temple Bar's pricier than most, but even they've got a different bit of fun that's distinctly "Ireland.".

My pretty little American girl seems to love it here, and I'm accidentally falling more in love with her with each passing second. I coax her away from Shannon, and Grace comes and sits at my side, cuddling close. Shannon rolls her eyes at me, but then goes and sits with Dermot doing much the same as me and my American girl. The others, Lily and Sean, cozy up, but they're not a real couple. They are, but they refuse to admit it to each other even if everyone else knows it. Not sure what else you can call it when you've been bedding the same girl for three years and invite her to everything, even family gatherings and Christmas, but they just say they're friends.

To each their own, I suppose. I'm not looking to do the same with my Grace Turner.

I feed her a thick cut chip from the group plate on table, grinning as she opens wide for me. She slides her tongue across the tip of the chip first before letting me slip the delicious morsel in her mouth so she can take a bite. I pop the other half into my mouth and chew it while we both stare at each other with a lick of lust in our eyes.

We're gonna keep that simmering for awhile now. Might be for a long while, too. I haven't kissed her twice yet so each of us is still safe for a time.

"Oi, what, do you need a room now?" Shannon asks us.

"Leave them be," Dermot says, nudging her, playful.

"Are ya offering?" I ask.

"I mean, I do have a hotel room, so..." Grace says, but then immediately turns to blushing, her cheeks a gorgeous ginger color.

"See? We're all set, Shannon. Thanks for your offer, though."

"I didn't mean it like that!" Grace says, laughing. "I'm definitely not inviting you back to my room. I barely even know you."

"He's truly terrible," Dermot says with a nod. "Don't let him in your room. He's like a stray. You'll never get rid of him and he'll expect you to feed him after that."

"True. I don't leave hair all over the place, though."

"Just in the shower drain," Shannon adds.

"That's *your* hair, and you leave it every time you and Dermot come stumbling to my door after drinking in the middle of the night. Keep your hair to yourself and use your own damn shower, woman."

"That rarely happens!" Shannon protests.

"Might have happened last week," Dermot reminds her.

"Still rare. When's the last time before that?"

"The week earlier?" I say.

"Two weeks in how many months, though?" she counters.

"You're not doing yourself any favors here, Shannon."

"Ugh. You two're teaming up on me. Lily! Help me with the--"

Except Lily's gone to a quiet corner to get her snog on with Sean and when the two of them start there's not much anyone can do to stop it.

"I think I'm gonna take a cue from them and steal my American girl away for a bit," I say, smirking over at Grace.

"You're going to drag me to a corner of the pub and make out with me?" she asks, half offended--her voice lifting--and the other half intrigued, her eyes aglimmer.

"Was thinking we'd try out some tried and true Irish pub sports," I say. "We'll see what happens from there."

"What, like rugby?" she asks.

"Oh, dear," Shannon says, shaking her head. "Don't even get them started, please."

"I still think we could do it," Dermot says, rushing his arms around, animated. "There's plenty of people in here to start up a match and if we're careful about it and add some rules it'd work."

"Aye, I'm sure of it, too," I say, nodding fierce to my best mate. "Next time!" To Grace, I ask, "How're you at darts?"

"Darts? Hm." She furrows her cute little brow and tosses her head to the side a little. "You throw the pointy part at the circle board, right?"

"That good, eh?" I ask with a smirk. "Let's make a friendly wager, shall we? I'll go easy on you."

"What should we wager?" she asks, that intrigued glimmer lighting her eyes a tempered steel blue once more.

"I'm not taking you to a corner to lock lips if that's what you're pulling at."

"What? Even if I win?" she says, pouting her adorable lips at me.

Please, Grace Turner. I'm having a hard enough time not kissing you as it is. Don't make it even worse for me. I'll never be able to let you go back to America if you keep this up.

Dermot and Shannon start whispering something or other. Probably about Grace and I, but I'm not gonna bother trying to figure that one out. I'm on a mission here. Win at darts, but not enough to annoy my alluring American girl.

"If I win, I get your phone number," I tell her.

"You don't even have her number yet?" Shannon shouts out, offended.

"Hush, Shannon!" Dermot says, laughing loudly at her.

"Fine," Grace says. "And if I win, you need to actually use it to call me."

"Oi, confident, are ya? I'll let you have that one, Grace Turner. Don't expect a phone call unless you win, though. I'll text you now and again, I suppose. Maybe a time or two."

"You'll text me constantly," she says, grinning wide. "I already know it. You can't hide the fact that you're madly in love with me, Dare Mackenzie. I can see it in your eyes."

"Yeah?"

"Show me this dart board of yours. Let's get to it."

"Aye, I will. I'll even let you go first. You know what you're doing?"

We stand up and I show her through the crowd to a barely quieter spot where the dart board's at. It's tucked in a corner, the board hanging from a wooden support beam holding up the ancient rafters. We fetch the darts and I sort them for her, handing her hers.

"You score points, right?" she asks, holding the dart like a cigarette, awkward and confused. "The middle part's good, isn't it?"

"You want me to go first and show you how it is?" I ask, deciding I ought to be a wee bit of a gentleman about this. Just a wee bit.

"I'm sure I'll figure it out," she says with a shrug. "How hard can it be?"

"Don't come crying to me when--"

And like a switch, Grace Turner's light suddenly coming on, she flips the dart around in her hand, holds it like a true pro, and flicks it at the board across from us. Her first dart lands clean and square right in the center.

"Ooh! What's that called again?" she asks, excited, hopping up and down. "A bullseye or something?"

"Oi, you're hustling me, aren't ya?"

"What, little ol' me?" she asks, batting her eyelashes at me.

Quick as a mouse, she tosses the other two darts, getting one in the circle just outside the center, outer bullseye, and then she goes for a bit of flourish, expertly aiming at the twenty inner ring.

Fuck me.

"You really want me to call you up, eh?" I ask, flashing her a cocky grin.

"I mean, I wanted to drag you to a corner and make out with you, but I've been told that's not an option..."

"And here I thought you were a good American girl," I say, shaking my head and taking my first shot. I nearly miss a bullseye, landing on the innermost circle instead. "What's up with that?"

"Aww, did you?" she asks, patting me lightly on the cheek after I take my second shot. "I'm very good at acting, remember? I'm in the drama club, so..."

My last dart lands well, but I'm still a few points behind this dirty little dart hustler.

"I can't believe this," I say, gathering my darts. "Some naughty little American girl's stolen my heart and it's all an act. I should've put up more defenses. I've been had."

"I'm really good at being naughty," Grace says in the most

proper good girl way possible. Oi. Fuck me again. "I'm a bad girl trapped in a good girl's body."

"Are ya now?" I ask, winking at her.

"Mhm..."

Suffice to say, I get my arse handed to me at darts after that. Begrudgingly, I offer up my phone so the feisty little minx can add her number to it.

"I'm, um... I'm not sure how it works, though," she says after typing in her number. "Like, international calling, you know? My phone doesn't really work here half the time and I haven't tried calling anyone and texts haven't been coming through, so..."

"Have you got WhatsApp?" I ask her. "That's an easier way of it. Can text and call and all sorts of other craziness."

She pulls out her phone and goes searching the appstore for WhatsApp. I show her how to connect to the pub's wifi to make this all the easier and then away she goes, downloading the app so I can call her up. She's won the privilege with her dart hustling, so she deserves that much. Deserves a lot more, too, even outside of the dart hustling.

"What's this other sort of craziness you mentioned?" she asks, lifting one brow.

"Oh, you know, the real dirty parts," I tell her, nonchalant. "You're the naughty one. I'm sure you know all about it."

"I don't, but I'm a quick learner," she says, nodding fast.

"Keen, eh?"

"Don't you judge me, Dare!" she says, laughing. "I'm just... curious..."

"Well, we can get real fancy and leave voice texts," I tell her. "Let's give it a shot. Stay here, yeah?"

She nods quick, waiting. I walk to somewhere a little quieter and private, then pull her up on WhatsApp and push the button to record a voice message.

GRACE

Anotification pops up on my phone. I've got a message. Is this like voicemail or how's that work? I open WhatsApp and look to see that I've got a chat request from none other than the infamous Dare Mackenzie. I've heard things about him, you know? He's a wild one. Acts a gentleman, but is truly a scoundrel. All that sort.

Dare I listen to it? I know I shouldn't. Nothing good can come of this. I...

I'm just making up stories in my head. Don't mind me.

Dare comes back, puts his hand on my hip like it belongs there, and glances down at me looking at my phone.

"What's this?" I ask him, pointing at the sound bar with a play button at the end.

"Well, you tap that little button there and you get to hear what I said. But if you don't, then it'll be a mystery. Like a voicemail message, but in a texty sort of form. Real fancy, let me tell you."

I push the button and then hold the phone to my ear like it's a secret, but, um...

Apparently the app defaults to something like speaker-phone and Dare's voice comes through loud and clear. Anyone and everyone can hear him. Oh my God, I hope he doesn't, um... is this going to be inappropriate? Oh gosh.

"Grace Turner, I want you to be the light of my life, so I can wake up every morning and do naughty dirty things to you, then go to bed every night with you at my side. Might be we'll wake up in the middle of the night and do some more naughty dirty things. Don't want to keep you up too much, though. How about a picnic now and then? Keep it fresh and sweet. This is what you get for hustling me at darts. Oi, look at how red your cheeks are now. Goodbye, beautiful."

I close the app fast and look around. I should have closed it earlier! What if someone heard everything? Ugh. Double ugh! Ugh ugh ugh. Dare's as rotten as his friends said, and also cute and sweet and sexy. I'd love to have gotten a message like that privately, but considering everyone around me probably heard it, um...

Yes, embarrassing or what?

"Wait, how'd you know my cheeks would be red?" I ask,

blushing shamelessly at him. It's not a secret or anything anymore.

"Lucky guess?" he asks, coy.

"You're awful," I say, turning so I can slap at his chest.

"True," he says, grinning at me. "Can you forgive me?"

"Maybe..." I say. "I want to hustle--I mean, beat--you at another game."

"I don't fall for the same tricks twice, Grace Turner," he says, laughing. "Let me guess, you're an expert at pool, too?"

"That's the one where you hit the balls with the long stick, right?" I ask, feigning innocence.

"Don't you start with me, woman," he says, pressing his forehead to mine, our noses touching.

"I want you to kiss me," I tell him, our lips inches away.

"Do you now?" he asks, smiling at me with his eyes.

"Yes. Please?"

"I told you what would happen if I kissed you twice," he says. "Are you ready for that?"

I wait. Is he going to do it? Should I do it instead? I know what he said, and I know how I feel, but... is it just talk, a bit of bluster, or is this real and true?

He kisses me. But on the nose. My heart melts and my legs tremble, weak. I didn't know I could be so affected by someone in such a short amount of time, but Dare Mackenzie makes me feel things. I know I can't, or I shouldn't, but I am, and I do, so...

"Let's talk after one of us wins," he says, smiling softly at me. "I think we're through with wagers, yeah? Seems like we're both interested in winning the same prize."

DARE

My pretty little American girl beat me at darts, and then she beats me at pool. I need to keep an eye on this one. If I were a gambling man, I'd have lost everything by now. She's already stolen the one thing I never planned to lose today.

My heart is yours, Grace Turner. You won it fair and square.

The pub's getting rowdier, but it's an Irish sort of rowdy where everyone's singing old songs, or new ones, and we're all having a grande time of it. Loud, but all of Ireland is loud on St. Paddy's Day. This is what my American girl came for and I'm glad she's enjoying herself.

I'm enjoying everything about her, too.

Dermot and Shannon and Lily and Sean are nearby singing their bloody hearts out in between stealing lovely glances at each other and a few quick kisses now and then.

Grace and I are doing a whole lot of the former, but the latter's gonna take a little more time.

Unfortunately it's time we don't have except for tonight.

"So, what's American university like?" I ask her. "College, yeah?"

"We call it college, but some places are universities," she says, smiling and cuddling closer to me. "It's... stressful. I mean, maybe it's not stressful for everyone, but it's stressful for me. I've always kind of been the type of person who puts their all into everything, and I think that's good, you know? Except it doesn't give me a lot of free time."

"Which is why you snuck away to Dublin," I say, smirking at her. "What made you think this was a good place to hide out?"

"St. Patrick's Day was always kind of a thing in my house growing up," she says with a tiny shrug. "Not as big as now, and probably not as big as a lot of places back home, but we'd make a little event out of it. My grandmother was Irish. Her great-grandfather came over a long time ago. It's not like everyone here who is obviously a lot more Irish than that, but in the United States people make a bigger deal out of it on St. Patrick's Day sometimes, which is fun. So we'd just have a nice dinner and celebrate in our own way. I can't drink or party back home, so I thought I'd combine my old memories with some nice new ones and be a little bad at the same time."

"A right naughty girl, for sure," I say, pressing my nose to her cheek, nearly forgetting myself and kissing her. "Not that naughty, though. You've done nothing wrong the whole time

I've been with you, Grace. Well, except letting me drag you around. Turned out fine though, yeah?"

"Ugh! I can't believe I let some strange Irish bad boy drag me through Dublin while I had the time of my life," she says, giggling and rolling her eyes at me. "It's not even that, though. Um... so, back home, the drinking age is higher, so if I had anything to drink and I got caught, well... I know people who do it and nothing bad happens, but in my mind it's still bad, you know? Except here it's legal, so it doesn't matter. I'm trying to be a bad girl but I still did it in a good girl way. I like to think I'm a work in progress, maybe. I could never do this back home, though."

"Yeah? What if I were there?" I ask, grinning at her. "Would you let me drag you out and get up to some mischief with me?"

"If *you* were there," she says, gazing into my eyes, all sweet and sexy, "I'd never get anything done. You're too charming, Dare. It's kind of intimidating sometimes. It's because I'm American, isn't it? If we were back home you'd be surrounded by American girls so you wouldn't even look twice at me, I bet."

"Are we making more bets?" I ask, finding her fingers, then her hand, and squeezing it tight. "You might have hustled me at darts and beat me at pool, but this is a bet you'll never win, Grace Turner. I wouldn't have to look twice. After I looked at you once my eyes would be glued to you for the rest of my life. Truth be told, they already are. Not sure I'll ever be able to look away from you."

"Shut up," she says, but without any of the harshness, her

soft, breathy sigh making her sound sweet as sin. She laughs a little, nervous. "What if you close your eyes? Would that help?"

"Should I try it?" I ask, poking out my tongue at her. "Like this?"

I close them, keep my eyes closed, and a half second later my girl sneaks close, leans in, and presses her lips to mine. I warned her, didn't I? You aren't as much of a good girl as you try to let on, love. You're pulling each of us into something I don't think either of us is ever going to be able to stop.

I kiss her back like she's the only one in the room. The singing fades away. All the light and the loudness vanishes, replaced by the feeling of two hearts beating together, two pairs of lips tasting each other's sweetness, two souls becoming one.

My free hand finds her cheek while the other squeezes tight to her hand. I caress along her cheekbone, fingers soft like feathers, enjoying the way she feels as we give our kisses to each other. Slow, cautious, her lips part and her tongue teases its way past my lips, tantalizing tenderness mixed with a throbbing desire.

I could kiss her like this for hours. I'd be hard the entire time, my cock desperately wanting release, but I could kiss Grace Turner softly and sweetly for hours at a time. I imagine I could do a whole lot of things with her for hours at a time, too.

Make love. Wander through the Dublin zoo. Sing bawdy songs in a pub. Kiss like it was the end of the world. Cuddle.

Sleep. Watch movies until the sunrise. Fuck hard. Break beds. Buy new ones. Buy a bed for a baby.

It takes both of us a second to realize it, but the singing's stopped, replaced by cheers from the corner. Letting love languish on our lips and in our souls, we slowly open our eyes and turn them towards the cheering. My old mates, her new ones, have stopped minding their own business and have decided to mind ours for us.

It's in jest, just teasing, but I love the way Grace's cheeks burn bright from it. And then I love the way that she ignores all of them, wraps her fingers in my hair, and pulls me back to her lips. We kiss again, harder, fervent.

There's my pretty little American bad girl. Not too bad. A little naughty now and then never hurt no one, though.

"You're beautiful," I tell her when we take a break from kissing. Everyone's found something better to do than cheer us and our kissing on, but honestly I wouldn't mind getting a roaring applause every time I kissed her, either.

"You've been drinking," she says, coy.

"You're still beautiful!" I say, laughing. "Aye, you've been drinking, too. Is that why you forgot my warning from earlier about kissing you twice?"

"I remember it perfectly well, Dare Mackenzie," she says, eyes staring hard into my soul. "I hope you remember it, too."

"I do," I tell her. "I will. Forever."

"Forever?" she asks, a hint of a teasing smirk, but a bit of worry knitting her brow.

"Forever," I say, repeating myself.

Shannon hops over from dancing with Dermot and sidles

up into a seat next to us. "I know you're both having fun snogging over here, but do ya wanna dance?"

"Oh no, how much has she drunk?" I ask Dermot, peering over Shannon's shoulder.

"Haven't kept track but I know it's been enough that I won't be able to stop her from dancing 'til tomorrow morning."

"All the dancing!" Shannon says, shouting it out to the whole pub, giddy and free.

"What'd'ya think?" I ask Grace.

"It's tradition," Shannon adds, nodding fast. "You know how to do a real Irish jig?"

"I haven't really ever tried," Grace says, smiling, on the verge of laughter. Shannon's joy is infectious once she really gets into it. "I think it'd be fun, though."

"That's the spirit!" Shannon says, taking Grace's hand and guiding her up. "Let's give it a go!"

GRACE

Shannon shows me the proper way to do an Irish jig in a pub, which is to say we hop about a lot and spin around and laugh and I'm not winning any awards for my dance skills right now but I'm having the time of my life.

Once I'm appropriately Irish jig-ified, Dare steps in and dances with me. He takes my hand and spins me around and we bounce, quick steps, to the live music blaring through the small pub. It's late. Later than I meant to stay out, to be honest. I don't know exactly what time it is as I'm scared to look at my phone and check, but the sky outside's no longer a cool afternoon or even a chill evening color. Dark black, with old shimmering lights shining down the streets, and the music from hundreds of little Irish pubs fills the night air just outside the lacquered wooden door at the front of the building.

Inside, it's just us, everyone who's left. As the night wears on, people slowly stumble out into the streets, but there's still a lot of us here, holed up and determined, dancing, laughing, drinking, and having a grand time.

Eventually the music dies off, all but one of the band members leaving. There's just a man sitting by himself, playing a ukulele, riffing together tunes from this song or that, nothing ever fully coming together, but a constant thrum that's distinctively reminiscent of the parade from earlier. Cozy and quaint and beautiful and nice.

A murmur shuffles through the rest of us left in the pub. Dare leads me to a seat, sits himself down, then pulls me into his lap.

"Hello, beautiful," he says, smiling at me. "We've a decision to make. It's lock-in shortly. What would you like to do?"

And... I have no idea? "What's lock-in?" I ask, scrunching up my brow.

"No lock-in in America?" he asks, a teasing little shake of his head. "Aye, I suppose not. Lock-in's when a pub shuts down for the night, can't let anyone else in, but if you're in before they lock the doors, you get to stay in and keep drinking for awhile. Like an encore at a concert, yeah? Except in this case it's staying around to keep having fun with your mates."

"Your mates look like they're about to pass out," I say, giggling.

We both look around at Dare's friends sitting scattered at various tables. Lily's mumbling, eyes half-closed, cuddled up with Sean. Shannon's trying to convince Dermot to wake up, and he's trying to convince her to let him lay his head in her lap. Eventually she relents and starts playing with his hair gently with her fingers and singing a quiet song to him. He looks up at her from her lap, enjoying his new pillow, and smiles brilliantly.

"So should we leave or do you want to stay?" Dare asks.

"Can we stay?" I ask him, afraid to give my true answer. I want to stay, to keep having fun, but I know he's probably tired, so...

"We can do anything you want to do tonight," he says, kissing me on the cheek, the press of his lips lingering as he pulls away.

"Aww. Just tonight?" I tease him, nibbling at my bottom lip and pleading with him with my eyes.

"Remember now, you're leaving me soon, Grace Turner," he says, hands wrapped around my tummy, pulling me closer to him. "Don't make me fall for you more than I already am."

"You should swim the Atlantic to see me again," I tell him, a fit of daring whimsy coming over me. "A grand romantic gesture."

"Aye, I could do that," he says, mischief glimmering in his emerald eyes. "Or I could try this newfangled thing. I think they call it flying. In a plane, yeah?"

"Not as grand," I say with a sigh and a wink.

"I'll make it up to you with a kiss?" he offers.

And he does. We kiss, and it's like all the other times we've kissed, except it's more, too. I want to do so much more than kiss my handsome Irish lover. I... I want to love him, for one. With all of me, everything. Body, soul, him naked atop me, me writing in ecstasy beneath him. I want to feel his warmth as he undresses me, feel the heat of his body and his eyes as he stares at me with the same fervent look he's given me all day.

I don't know why, but I fully believe that Dare Mackenzie is in love with me. It's easy to believe because I'm in love with him, too.

Why did we let things go this far?

I meant to be naughty for the weekend, but I never meant to be *this* naughty. I never meant to give my heart away to a stranger, never meant to steal his in return, and...

"One more dance," I say, whispering into his ear. "Please?"

"I'd dance with you until the end of all time, Grace Turner," he says.

We dance, but like all good things, this night has to come to an end at some point.

Or...

Does it really?

Have to end, I mean.

I wish it didn't.

Maybe it doesn't...

DARE

I take my pretty little American girl out of the pub, sneaking our way out the back. It's a little more fun that way. I wanted to give her a taste of lock-in, and while tonight's been wilder than most, to be honest we usually don't sneak out the back. Just seemed like a fun way to make it funner, yeah?

She looks around, acting like we're committing a crime, peeking about for any sign of the authorities.

When her head's turned one way, I jump back like we've been caught in the act.

"Oh, shite!" I shout out to an empty alleyway.

"We didn't do it!" Grace screeches at the non-existent police.

Then she stares through the darkness at nothing for half a second before turning her evil eyed gaze my way. She waves her finger at me like she's about to cast a curse with her witch's wand.

Nose scrunched up as hard as can be, she gives me a real piece of her mind. "You're awful, Dare Mackenzie! Absolutely horrible! You nearly scared me half to death! Don't do that!"

"There's no need to sneak around," I tell her, laughing and wrapping my hand about her hip, pulling her to my side. "Let's get you back to your hotel, tuck you in real good, I'll give you a kiss on the forehead, and then I'll be on my merry way so you can dream of me something fierce."

"Oh, you *wish*," she says, but she cuddles closer to me, putting her arm around me, too.

"Where're we going, sweetling?" I ask her.

"Um, my hotel's kind of a ways outside of the city center, but it's not too far. I think I can figure out how to get back there from here. I like this one, because..."

But she trails off, holding her words. No worries. Makes no difference to me. I want to see what she likes about it no matter what it is.

"I'd like to see why you like it," I tell her, stopping to smile and look into her eyes.

"I... I don't think I can invite you back to my room, though," she adds, our eyes and our souls locked together as one. "It wouldn't be appropriate."

"No no, not at all appropriate," I say, nodding my head in agreement. "Not sure I could handle myself properly if you did, so... it's for the best, Grace."

GRACE

We find our way back to my hotel, a quiet and cozy walk. Dare holds me tight for half of it, but it's not exactly the easiest way to walk, so in the end we settle for holding hands the rest of the way. My hand feels so small and perfect in his. He squeezes every so often, for no reason at all, just to remind me that this is real, that we're actually doing this, right here and now, and that somehow despite the odds we've found each other during this amazing day leading up to this perfect moment.

The looming white facade of my hotel peeks into view, white granite columns lining the front, with tall windows rising up behind them. The first time I saw it I thought of an ancient Roman castle, something odd and in contrast with the rest of Ireland but somehow fitting so well with everything around it.

We walk along the long cobblestone walkway that leads

straight to the front entrance, sleepy trees barely budding along our path, darkness and stars shining through their slim branches. The front of the hotel curves with the path, almost imperceptible, like someone designed the hotel to fit along-side the stone walkway that just so happened to be there instead of the other way around.

"It's beautiful," Dare says as we start our final journey along the cobblestone track. "I can see why you'd like it."

"It really is, but... can I show you something?" I ask him, hoping to stave off some of the finality of tonight.

"Aye," he says, smiling over at me. "Anything."

We sneak around to the side, to this small archway covered with green and vines. A scattering of lights shines through the end of the garden tunnel, pulling us towards it like love bugs to a bright light. At the end of the tunnel through the archway, a garden like something out of Alice in Wonderland opens up, with tables and wrought-iron chairs and little stone decorations everywhere.

"They have a secret garden!" I say, squealing with delight.

Yes, um... I squealed the first time I saw the secret garden online in pictures, and then the second time when I saw it for the first time in person, and... basically every time after that. I've seen it quite a few times now and I can't stop squealing about it. Sorry, but I'm not even remotely sorry!

"Shall we sit?" Dare asks me, nodding to a table and chairs.

"Um... no, um... I want to show you something else I like, too," I say, unable to meet his gaze. I look everywhere but right at him, and then everywhere else except for at a particular window on the third floor that looks out over the middle of the hidden garden.

Dare clears his throat, a slight cough, and nods to me. I squeeze his hand and pull him towards the doorway alongside the garden that leads to the rear of the hotel. We skip past the lobby, direct to the elevators, and slowly step past the threshold inside the open door. The elevator door closes, trapping us in. I press the button for the third floor.

"Do you always stay in such fancy places?" Dare asks, teasing me as we take our short ride up.

"It's not that fancy, is it?" I ask, self-conscious. "It's... I just liked it. I stay in a lot of hotels for school. Because of sports and stuff like that. I think they're really interesting. I like the ones that have character and this one is special and unique. I don't know if I'd call it fancy, but..."

"Secret gardens are a bit fancy," Dare says, but he softens his teasing with a kiss on my cheek.

"I'll be fancy all I want, Dare Mackenzie," I tell him, leaning into his kiss. "I'm naughty for the weekend, remember? I can do what I like."

"Oi, that's the spirit, my pretty little American bad girl."

"Am I yours or are you mine?" I counter.

The elevator door opens and I hop outside quick, still holding his hand. I tug him along with me and he comes, smiling wide the entire time.

"What're you showing me now?" he asks as we walk down the darkly decorated hall, a stark contrast to the crisp white exterior.

A mix of triangles and other sharp shapes line the walls,

deep greys and dark blacks, with a weave of lines streaking through the carpet at our feet. It looks like some kind of graph after you punch in an abstract mathematical equation on a calculator. Every door we pass is made of glossy dark wood, each with its own smooth plaque indicating the room number.

I stop outside of room 323. My hand trembles as I reach into my jacket pocket for my room key. Silent, Dare stands beside me as I swipe the key against the keycard panel set in the door. A light on the panel flashes green as the lock in the door clicks.

"My room," I say, slowly taking the handle in my hand, pulling down even slower, pushing it open. "I... I want to show you my bed..."

DARE

My pretty little American girl's fingers tremble on the door latch as she looks at me, eyes wide, pupils slowly filling, becoming beautiful and big, anticipation mixed with excitement.

"I... I want to show you my bed..." she says, her voice nary a whisper.

I reach out and place my hand atop hers on the door. She lets loose the latch and I take her fingers in between mine. The door closes just as slowly as it opened a few whiles earlier, a definitive click breaking through the thick silence between us.

"Do you now?" I ask her, my voice soft, steady, a breath of a kiss and nothing more. "You won't regret it, will you? I want to come in, Grace. I'd do just about anything in the world to spend the night with you, but..."

Aye, and maybe I'm ruining my chances here. Possibly I'm

giving up the moment of a lifetime. Is it worth leaving when I might spend a wild, intimate night filled with love and passion, sweat and desire? If this is it, if this is the only time we'll ever have together for an entire lifetime, then neither of us should waste even a second, but if there's something more, if there could be more, I'd give up anything to have it, even this.

Yeah, I've found myself in a right pickle of a situation, eh? Fuck, I don't even like pickles that much.

Grace Turner looks at me with those lovely wide eyes of hers, never one to turn down a challenge. She's marriage material if I ever saw it, the girl I'll be dreaming of for the rest of my life. Will she wake up at my side after those dreams or will she always be the one who got away?

"I'm not saying anything, Dare Mackenzie," she says, pushing close to me, almost a hug, our bodies touching as she tucks her chin low and presses her cheek to my chest. "I know how you feel and if you don't know how I feel right now then maybe it's best if you don't come in, because--"

Now now, beautiful. We can't have you talking like that...

I take her chin in my hand and pull her up to look in her eyes. I only need a second, so that's all I take. Both our eyes close, both of us knowing what's coming next. I touch my lips to hers, soft at first, but needing more quicker than I ever have before. She clings to me, her room key still clenched in her hand as she grabs my shirt. I wrap my arm around her, squeezing her tight, needing to feel her heat and her body touching me.

Then, wordless, I take her keycard and tap it to the door.

Eyes closed, kissing the woman of my dreams, the one I want to love forever, I pull down the latch and push the door open. I hold it with my foot and lifting her up into my arms, grabbing her ass as she wraps her legs around me.

Desirous, frantic, we kiss, stumbling into her room. I carry her inside. One eye peeking open, I flip the switch to turn the lights on. Grace peeks one eye open, too, watching me. She giggles and I laugh as the door shuts behind us and I squeeze her ass tight, dragging her to the bed.

"Aye, this is a bed, alright," I say, standing at the foot of it.

She looks over her shoulder, eyeing it admirably. "It's very comfortable," she says.

"Is it now?" I ask. "So you're saying if I set you down you're gonna fall asleep on me?"

"Noooooo," she says, shaking her head fast. "Well, not right away. After, maybe. If you'll stay with me?"

"What kind of gentleman would I be if I didn't stay with you on your last night in Dublin?" I say, teasing her with a kiss on the cheek.

"A very poor gentleman indeed," she says, nodding fast. "So now you have to do it."

"Can't even make me leave," I tell her, grinning.

"You know what else is comfortable?" she asks.

"Tell me?"

"I mean... I think it is, but... getting into bed naked is a lot more comfortable than wearing clothes."

"Is it now?" I ask, furrowing my brow, acting surprised. "Huh."

"Here," she says. "I'll show you."

GRACE

I squirm out of Dare's arms, sliding my butt onto the bed. He stands at the foot, watching me with fire and patience in his eyes. We're going to take this slow, but once we get started I think all bets are off.

I slide his denim jacket down his shoulders first, letting it slip to the patterned carpet. My fingers press against the buttons of his button-down shirt, undoing them one by one, top to bottom. Once I have the front all the way open, I take a second to admire his tone, his abs, his chest tensing slightly as I rake my fingers across his muscles. He smiles down at me, teasing his hand across my cheek and brushing my hair back behind my ear.

"This needs to come off," I tell him with a nod, pushing his shirt off his shoulders.

"Does it now?" he asks, helping me slide his shirt the rest of the way down his arms and to the ground.

I wrap my fingers around his bicep, or at least as much as I can. I think it'd take three hands for me to go all the way around it, and unfortunately I only have two. Not that that's going to ruin my fun, though. I tease my fingernails down his arms, the small hairs on his forearm rising as I enjoy every inch of his muscles.

"Seems to me we're not very equal here," Dare says, biting his bottom lip as he stares down at me.

"Oh?" I ask, coy and sweet. "How so?"

While my hand teases and toys with his strong forearm, he unzips my bomber jacket and then peels it back behind me. I take my hand away from my newfound fun for a moment so he can help me out of my jacket, and when I try to go back to his forearm he tugs me out of my shirt, too.

I sit on the bed, looking up at him, eyes wide, my risque choice of a lacy black bra the only thing between me and pure toplessness.

"A true bad girl, I see," Dare says, eyes glued to the tops of my breasts.

"I didn't wear this for you, Dare Mackenzie," I tease him. "I wore it for me. Don't get so excited."

"Look straight a second and I'll show you how excited I am, Grace Turner," he says, fingers tucked beneath my chin, leading me to look straight and...

He's standing in front of me, pants still on, a proud erection pressed hard against the front. I can see a perfect outline of his cock, starting in the center of his pants, then dragging slowly to the side, bold, bulging, and throbbing.

Oh. My. God.

I can't look away. Not only that, my fingers have a mind of their own right now. I want to touch it. I need to. I unbutton his pants as he strokes my cheek with his thumb. I pull the waistband of his pants down, revealing a pair of tight trunks, made even tighter by the fact that his glorious cock is bulging against them.

Dare kicks off his shoes, helps me slide his pants down the rest of the way to his feet, and kicks those off, too.

"You can look, Grace Turner, but you can't--"

Teasing. A joke. I can't even begin to imagine he doesn't want to be touched right now. I also can't even remember what I'm doing or what he just said. My fingertips slip under the waistband of his trunks, tugging them down until his cock pops free from its tight confines. One hand wraps around his shaft, stopping every single other word he was about to say, point blank.

Instead, a growls out a guttural moan, throaty and full of lust. I stroke his cock, licking my lips at the slick precum coating the head.

"Mine," I say, claiming him for my own.

His eyes roll into the back of his head as his chin rises towards the ceiling. I'll get no challenge to my claim from him. Not now, and maybe not ever.

While Dare is properly distracted, and because I've decided to be a very bad girl right now—befitting of my weekend plans, right?--I slip my tongue out and run the tip up and down the tiny slit on the head of his cock. Slow, stroking him with both my hands, I lap and lick up and down, tasting his arousal.

Sweet musk, like leather and vanilla connected, heady and intoxicating. I want more. I slide my tongue across my lips, coating them in a mix of his precum and my enthusiastic desire, before parting them slightly and taking him into my mouth. Dare groans loudly, his fingers wrapping into my hair, taking a fistful.

Rough, yet wonderfully gentle, he pulls me onto his cock. Slow and delicious, my lips slide down his shaft, my tongue tracing a slick line across the underside of his cock. He pulls me as far as he can until the tip of his cock taps against the back of my throat, and then he coaxes me a little more. I swallow, trying to take more of him in my mouth. A little more, but still far too much to fit. I can't take all of him, but I can get this last little bit, just one inch more, the fingers of one hand still wrapped firmly around the base of his shaft showing me how much I have left to take.

I breathe through my nose, swallowing, his cock vibrating in the back of my throat. Pulsing in my mouth, throbbing with desire, his fingers fisting my hair, holding me as deep as I can go.

I want more. I've never wanted something this badly in my entire life. Being the bad girl I know I can be, I let go of his cock and grab a handful of his ass in each hand. Leverage. This is a math problem in the making. For every action, there's an equal and opposite reaction.

In this instance, the action is me pulling myself further against Dare's cock, and the equal and opposite reaction is that I somehow manage to slide another inch of him down my throat.

"Holy fucking hell," Dare grunts out, his cock twitching and throbbing, pulsing, pounding. "If ya keep that up you're gonna--"

I'm a bad girl, Dare Mackenzie. Real bad. You're about to find out just how bad I can be, too.

Keeping one handful of his ass in my hand, I reach the other one back and grab his overfull balls, palming them. We need to fix this. These shouldn't be so full. He's probably been working himself up all night by teasing me, and I think he deserves a reward for it, don't you?

I massage his balls in my palm, coaxing and urging him to release his pent up desire. I don't think this was my plan when we first came in my room, but now that I've started I can see just how easy it is to be a bad girl. Don't think. Just give in to the desire.

Not with everyone. Just with Dare. He deserves to see my wild side in action. I want to be even more naughty when I'm with him. I...

His balls tense up. I lightly massage them, goading him to give me what I want, milking him for my own desires. I can barely breathe, but that's beside the point. I've got a perfectly good nose and that's good enough for now. I take in a sharp breath, my nostrils flaring, cool air surging down my throat and pressing against the head of Dare's cock at the same time. I swallow, and lick at the underside of his shaft. My eyes start to water and grow wider, excited, as he spasms in my mouth.

No longer a pulse or a throb, oh no. This is an uncontrollable shake, a constant thrum, pleasure jolting from his balls to the base of his shaft, to where my tongue is massaging and teasing him, and then...

The head of his cock throbs against the back of my throat, swelling thicker and bigger. I don't even have a chance to taste him before he spills jet after jet of cum directly down my throat. I feel the sticky sweetness like honeyed candy as I swallow, and every time I swallow he throbs and grows even more in my mouth.

I milk him for every drop he's worth until he's still gently throbbing in my mouth but nothing more is sliding down my throat. His leg twitches and he starts to laugh, giddy and unexpected. I lick under his shaft slow, tickling him, and he laughs even more. Joyous, handsome, and the most lovely man I've ever laid eyes on, Dare Mackenzie is completely wrapped around my finger and I love it.

I love him.

I slide back as soon as he lets my hair loose, letting his cock slip out of my mouth with a pop as I smack my lips against the head of his cock. He stares down at me like I'm some sort of fallen angel who came crashing down from the heavens for him and him alone.

I stare up at him, more than a little self-satisfied, licking my lips.

"Mmmm," I murmur, our eyes locked. "Told you I was a bad girl."

DARE

"I'll never doubt you again," I say, unable to stop smiling. "You feckin' drained me. My God."

Grace stares up at me with a cute little smirk plastered on her lips, her cute little arse still seated on the edge of the bed. Remnants of my cock having been in her mouth cover the side of her lip, a slip of saliva trailing down the corner towards her chin.

"I... I don't usually do that..." she mumbles, some of her previous self-confidence slipping away.

"Aye, not usually?" I ask, staring down at my still rock hard cock. "Grace, you broke me."

"What! I did not!" she says, laughing as she looks at the hard, complicated problem between my legs.

Without warning, she runs her fingers across the top of my cock, then pushes it down, giggling as it bounces back up immediately.

"Broken," I say, shaking my head. "Feckin' broke, that's what you did. It's still up. You drained me. Felt like I was coming undone from the inside out with your little swallowing tricks. You don't usually do that, yeah? Holy feckin' hell, I want you to do it again, but..."

"But what?" she asks, eyes wide, tossing a curious, sidelong glance at my newfound permanent erection.

Don't you worry about me. We'll get this fixed soon enough. I know a trick or two for getting rid of an erection, Grace Turner. Involves peeling off those ripped jeans of yours and seeing what you've got on underneath before burying myself deep inside you and making you feel the way you've just made me feel.

Soon. She's leaving tomorrow, but we've still got all night, and I plan on making good use of it.

I swagger over to the side of her room, dim from the lack of lights, with a tall wooden cupboard tucked in the corner.

"That's, um..."

"Come here, Grace Turner," I say, turning to her. "I need your help."

As she scurries up off the bed to join me, I swing open the door of the cupboard, revealing the minibar. The fridge is nice and handy, but that's not what I'm about right this instant. I scan through the nips of alcohol, my finger waving over them like an adult game of duck, duck, goose.

And... aye, there we go.

"You ever tried this?" I ask her, hoisting up a bottle of Patron XO Cafe.

"I told you I'm a good girl, Dare Mackenzie!" she says, acting all cute and affronted.

"Aye, you flip flop a whole lot, Grace Turner. First you're a good girl, then you're a bad girl, now you're a good girl again? I'm gonna need you to make up your mind, beautiful."

"I'll be bad tonight," she says, scooting close, purring in my ear. "Just for you, because... just because."

"Because I'm madly in love with you and going to make you my wife," I say with a self-assured nod.

"Shush!" she says, laughing and nuzzling her cheek against me. "You're awful. You make me want to do things I would never do in a million years."

"We're not being too bad, yeah?" I ask, kissing her forehead quick. "Aside from you milking every last drop of cum from my balls. Good God, woman. How am I supposed to return the favor now?"

"I can think of a few ways..." she whispers, her fingers creeping out and tapping against my firm erection.

"I'm gonna need you to calm yourself," I say, grinning at her. "I need to distract you a second, too. Share this with me, love?"

"What is it?" she asks, eyeing the little bottle. "Tequila?"

"Aye, and coffee liqueur. A tried and true Irish liquor if I ever knew one."

"Tequila's not Irish!" she says, her eyes casting a dirty glare my way. "And coffee this late? You're trying to keep me up all night, aren't you?"

"Shite. She's on to me," I say to the room.

"I'll try it..." she says, stepping up on tiptoes to kiss me on the cheek. "Just this once. Because after this I'm going to be a good girl again, and if you can't handle that, well..."

"I'll handle you every which way I can get you," I tell her before cracking open the little bottle.

There's not much. This is a nip of alcohol we're talking about. Damn. Calm yourself. I take a sip, downing half of it, then hold it up to her lips so she can drink the rest. It's smoother than tequila has any right to be, a hint of bitter with a dash of sweet.

She licks her lips after and smiles at me. "You know what that would go good with?"

"What's that?" I ask, curious.

"A pint of Guinness."

"Your Irish is showing, love," I say, smirking.

"What! It's true. It'd be good, I bet."

"Aye, a good way to get drunk off your arse."

"Well, we're not doing that," she says, shaking her head. "I was promised a proper manhandling, Dare Mackenzie. I'm waiting."

"There's a shot you might like," I say, a little storytelling time while I guide her back to bed. "You mix the Cafe Patron with some Bailey's and then down her just like that. Baby Guinness, they call it. So, aye, you're definitely onto something."

"See?" she says, excited. "Maybe I should be a bartender. Could help pay for school during the summer."

"Summer's soon, yeah?" I say, asking the obvious.

"Um, pretty soon."

"You get the whole thing off?"

"Kind of. I mean, there's a lot I have to do still. We have volleyball practice during the summer, and there's prep for the upcoming year with the drama club and planning out all the plays we're going to perform, bringing in new freshman and all that, and... I have time off, but it's not enough."

"Not enough to come visit me," I say, stating the obvious.

We're getting even more obvious by the second, but I'm holding a bit of my own obvious back before I go too wild and crazy. Grace Turner's got a wild streak longer than a winding Irish road in the countryside, but she'll never be a true bad girl. She's gooder than gold, and that's one of the things I love about her.

"That would be really nice," she says, wistful. "I... I could try. You could come visit me, too? Do you--"

"I'm gonna cut you off right there, love," I say, shaking my head. "That's talk for tomorrow or the day after or a week from now, or sometime in the future. Right now's time for something else."

My cock's still harder than the Cliffs of Moher and it's been an elephant in the room this entire time, just sticking up straight while I'm sitting here trying to have a gentle conversation on the bed with the woman I swear to God I'm going to marry one day.

Not today, but that doesn't mean we can't start practicing for our wedding night, yeah?

I roll over on top of her, pressing my lips tight to hers,

keeping her words at bay, distracting her with a promise of a lot more to come. I reach down with one hand and undo the buttons of her jeans, unzipping them quick, then kissing my way down her body.

Her throat is so kissably soft I almost distract myself from my goal, but then I manage to pull myself lower.

Reaching behind her, I unsnap her bra and peel it off, my eyes soon glued to the gloriously pert breasts right in front of me. She's got an athlete's body, that's for sure, but nothing too hard, just the right amount of softness to sink your teeth into. Her nipple fits perfectly between my lips and her other breast is a perfect handful for my palm. Perfect all the way 'round. I sink my teeth in, as it were, both enjoying every last taste of her, but also nibbling lightly at her nipple, reveling in the subtle little moans she lets out as her body starts to wriggle and writhe beneath me.

I fucking love the way she squirms. She's responsive as sin, in tune with everything I want, need, and desire. I could play with her breasts for days if I had the chance, but we'll have to wait on that for another time.

One hand palming her breast, I kiss my way down her stomach. Small pecks mixed with licks, playful nips, a tickle or two. She squirms even more, laughing and giggling as I play with her body, exploring every last inch.

When I get to her hips, I kiss her hipbone lightly, teasing a trail from the outside in. I wrap my fingers into the waistband of her jeans and her panties and pull them down all together. She's mine now, laying on the bed, bare to me, intimate skin soft and slick, wet and perfect.

"Dare..." she murmurs, her fingers teasing into my hair, tugging lightly, toying with me like I've been toying with her.

"Aye, beautiful," I say, licking my lips at the goddamn beautiful sight right before my eyes. "I know what you want. Don't you worry. You're about to get everything you've ever dreamed of."

GRACE

My mind goes blank and my eyes clench shut as Dare presses his lips against my wet, pulsing clit. I've been aroused for longer than I can remember. I knew it when we were in his friend's apartment, but I thought it'd pass soon enough. Just a flit of attraction, you know? Nothing more.

But it was more. It was always more. It kept growing into more the longer we spent together. More and more, becoming an insatiable need, a desire that was impossible to quench.

This wasn't something I could just go home and pull out my vibrator for. This was a deeper hunger, a craving for everything Dare had to offer, whether I wanted to admit it or not.

And... more than that, too. But we promised we wouldn't talk about it right now. I don't even know if I can think about the future at the moment. My mind is less than fully functional and it's fading into ecstasy with every passing fraction of a second.

He kisses my clit, soft and sweet, then teases his lips away, kissing up along the other side of my hipbone. I squirm and writhe, instinctively trying to grind up against him, but he's too far away and it's not enough.

"Calm down, my pretty little American girl," he says in that sweet Irish accent of his.

That is one-hundred percent not the way to get me to calm down, Dare Mackenzie...

...And he absolutely knows it, too, the asshole.

His middle finger appears out of nowhere, sliding up and down between my slick folds. Oh! I... I like that. My puffy, greedy lips kiss at his fingertip, wet and needy, but he refuses to give me more. Kissing his way back to my clit, he slides his tongue out, pressing the tip against my sensitive pearl.

In some sort of one-two combination, he glides his finger inside me right as he starts licking my clit, teasing his tongue in a gentle circle around the inside of my hood. A tease, an aching desire, his tongue circling the hood of my clit, then more, an urgent tap, licking up and down across my pulsing, throbbing, eager clit.

As if that wasn't the worst of it, his finger slides into me easily, curling up and hooking inside me. He seesaws like that, grinding and gripping the rough spot just up and inside my pussy, forcing a surge of passion and a sense of fulfillment deep inside me.

I'm far too aroused for my own good and Dare quickly realizes it. He slides in one more finger next to the first, solidifying his grip on my pleasure. And... oh my God, this is what I've been waiting for. Or at least close enough for now. I've wanted his cock inside me since before I pulled it out of his pants, but I've kind of just wanted *him* inside me for, oh... I don't know... let's just ignore that question because I've been trying not to be too much of a bad girl tonight and basically I'm completely failing at holding onto my good girl side right now.

Rocking back and forth, his fingers pressed tight inside me, not too fast, not too slow... just perfectly right in all the most amazing ways... I writhe and squirm with him, becoming a puppet to his masterful control.

He feeds into my passion. I felt this way when I had his cock in my mouth, but I think maybe it was a little bit of the reverse. Not quite, because I still felt pleasure--his pleasure-- in a way I couldn't really explain. But now I feel him and my pleasure. It's... it's a lot.

He growls against my pussy, his lips vibrating against mine as he laps and licks at my clit. His fingers rock a little faster as I start to clench and grind against him. My body gives itself to him, soul, essence, and desire. Ecstasy imminent. Every last ounce of me trying to hold back completely vanishing as he overtakes me in every sense of the word.

My mouth opens, but I don't know how to speak. A sharp scream of something slips from my lips, words I can't even explain or define.

"I... oh my God, Dare, soon, I'm..."

He answers with his own desires, keeping a steady pace, fingers rocking inside me, filling me, pressing pleasure into the deepest core of my desire. His tongue is the sinful cherry on top, forcing my orgasm to the fore, pushing me to greater heights of intimate ecstasy.

I cum. Hard. Slick and wet, my entire body spasming, muscles I barely knew existed becoming tight, squeezing harder than I ever thought possible. He drains me like I drained him, desiring me in a way no one ever could have before.

I don't have a ton of experience here, but even I know this isn't the kind of sex that just everyone has with a one night stand they met earlier that day. This is so much more. It's incomprehensible. My brain is numb and my body is a wreck, sore and aching and alive with desire and need. I want to run a marathon and sleep for a week all at the same time.

Dare keeps teasing and tormenting me until it's too much. I laugh and squirm, trying to get away from him. He licks my clit one last time, sending a trill of giggles that echo through my core, and then he slides up and away from me, his lips slick with my arousal.

Oh, I want to kiss him. Is that weird? I... I just...

I wrap my arms around him and pull him close to me and rain kisses all over his cheeks and his lips and every part of him that I can get. I forget that we're naked in bed. I forget that he had an impossibly hard erection even after I made him cum earlier.

I forget all of this until I don't, because as easily as if we're made for each other, once our lips touch again in a kiss, the head of Dare's cock finds a perfect fit right between the lips of my pussy, and he slides in like we were made for each other.

"I want every damn piece of you, Grace Turner," he says, grunting into my kiss, slowly thrusting into me as deep as he can. "Every. Fucking. Thing. All of you."

"Then take me," I say, whispering against his lips, my eyes wide, excited, gazing into his with a heavy lid of ecstasy.

DARE

The first second I'm inside her is like a warm summer sunset in Galway while looking out at the Atlantic from atop one of the slippery rocks on a cozy road alongside the ocean. Aye, and if I'm not careful I'm gonna fall right in, too. I've already fallen, Grace Turner. There's no turning back. Don't let me be the only one, beautiful.

She whimpers beneath me, a pretty little whisper of a sound sneaking out from between those plump, rosy lips of hers. I want to kiss her so bad, so I do. I press my lips to hers, tasting her sounds, feeling the vibrations rocking through my lips as I feel the clench and throb of her post-orgasmic pussy wrapped around my cock.

"Can you handle this?" I ask, teasing her with a gentle nibble to her lower lip. "I haven't worn you out now, have I?"

"Shut up," she says, peeking one eye open, refusing to even acknowledge me with the both of them.

"That's a good girl," I say, pushing deep inside her. She lets out a little gasp as I bottom out, my balls pressed tight against her slick lips.

"No," she says, shaking her head as I pull out of her. "I'm being very naughty right now, Dare."

"Are ya?" I ask, smiling, my lips to hers. "How naughty can I be with you?"

"Mmm?" she mumbles, lazily opening her eyes halfway, looking at me through the dim darkness, only a single light on shining in the entryway of her hotel room.

I pull back, watching her pout as our lips stop touching. Grinning at her, I grab her hips, pulling her up, angling her on my cock just the way I want her to take it. When I feel the telltale grip, that slight little pop that says I'm in exactly the right spot, I rock against her, sliding her back and forth on my cock while I stay deep inside her sinfully perfect pussy.

Her eyes grow wide, no longer hazy and half-lidded, and she grabs at the bedspread with her hands, fingers turning pale and white from her tight grip.

Aye, there we go, Grace Turner. I'll show you how naughty we can be together...

GRACE

Dare is, dare I say, um... big. Throbbing. Thick. His cock slides deeper inside me than I've ever felt before. I'm all about the motion of the ocean and all that, but Dare knows how to use what he's working with, and he's not only got the moves down, but technically oceans are pretty big, so...

Look, he's got a big cock. And that's not why I'm sleeping with him. But since we're here I'm going to enjoy myself, alright? Don't judge me.

I'm a bad girl for the weekend. Naughty as sin. Steamy. Dirty. And, well...

At first I think he just wants to admire my body while he thrusts inside me, and I can't say I wouldn't enjoy that. There's something about the way he looks at me, even when I have clothes on, that sends me into overdrive. Now that we're naked, shadows wrapped around us, accenting every curve, the muscles all along his body, my hips, his abs, the two of us together completely.

Yes. Give me that look, Dare Mackenzie. I want to see the lust in your eyes. I want you to know exactly what you do to me exactly while you're doing it.

And... oh shit. We, um... we forgot something...

Right when I have that thought, Dare grabs my hips, slides me up his thighs slightly, and starts rocking inside me. There's a new sensation of deepness, a sudden fullness that's even fuller than before. And if that wasn't enough, the way he has me angled makes my clit slide up and down his lower abs with each pull and rock.

He holds my hips tight, focusing on the rhythm, building speed until our bodies are a clap of flesh and sin, his cock as deep inside me as it can go, vanishing between my slick lower lips. Maybe even deeper. I don't know what he's doing to me or how he's doing it, but it's like I've been completely filled up, then filled again. My clit aches with pleasure and desire, my body having just orgasmed but desperately wanting to cum hard again and again for him.

I've never done that before. Never had more than one orgasm. Not by myself, and not with anyone else. It's not like it just stops feeling good or anything, but after the first time it's like an elusive pleasure that seems just out of reach, and...

Not sure how out of reach it'll be for much longer if Dare keeps this up.

"Dare, I..." I say, somehow managing to mumble out his name.

He looks at me with love and lust in those scorching

emerald eyes of his. I can't look away. We look into each other's souls as our bodies come together, both of us on the brink of something powerful and amazing.

I let out a primal moan, my mind instinctively knowing how to be his before I even realize it. I'm still lost, not sure exactly what we're doing, but, oh, do I want to do it. Yes. Please. All of it. Oh my God. I...

A second orgasm crashes through me, deep inside me. My pussy wraps around his cock like a vice, refusing to let go. He slides me up and down, rocking my clit across his core, his taut lower abs, sending me higher and higher, refusing to let me fall from this passion too fast or too far.

It's a lot. This is a lot to take in. Maybe too much. It's more than I can handle right now, but I don't want it to ever stop. A starburst of light flares behind my clenched shut eyelids, a story of passion and love and fireworks unfolding. It pushes deep inside my core, then floods through the rest of my body. My mind is the last to go. I lose all thoughts for what seems like forever or a fraction of a second. Timeless and no time at all.

When I open my eyes, everything is bright and vivid even through the dim darkness of my barely lit hotel room. It's like I can see colors that I've never seen before, never knew existed, and this is what life and love with Dare would be like. This is what it *is* like. We're experiencing it right now. Together.

Except...

"Cum," I whisper to him. Then louder. "Cum inside me. It's... it's alright, Dare. I..."

He doesn't need me to tell him twice. He pushes hard against my pubis, our bodies becoming even more entwined than before, and he lets loose everything he's been holding back. His cock thrashes inside me, wild, a throbbing spasmic mess of pleasure. I can feel him as he cums inside me, deep. I feel his warmth and sticky wetness mixing with my own slickness, the aftermath of my orgasmic bliss.

Once he's finished cumming deep inside me, he slowly crashes atop me, wrapping his arms around me, cradling me in a tight embrace.

"Fuck," he says, the word sounding perfect right about now.

"Fuck," I agree, grinning and laughing and kissing his cheeks.

"I should've grabbed a condom, eh?" he says, a hint of guilt in his voice.

"Well, yes," I say, rubbing my nose against his. "But you promised you're going to love me forever and I have an IUD, so... don't break our promise."

"I'll never break my promise to you, Grace Turner," he says, honest and true.

"So that means you're going to swim the Atlantic to come see me?" I ask, teasing him, giving him a quick peck on the cheek.

"Aye. Should I start now?" he asks, a mischievous glimmer in his emerald eyes. "It's a long swim."

"Noooo," I say, latching my arms around him and clinging to him like a bug. "You can't leave. You need to stay in my bed. I need you."

"Oi, you need me that much already?" he asks, kissing me quick on the nose.

"Aye," I say, stealing his word.

"And will we be having breakfast together tomorrow morning?"

"Aye," I say again, nodding fast.

"And..."

"Aye."

"You didn't even let me ask the question that time!" he says, laughing.

"Aye!" I say, giggling with him. "Shut up and kiss me."

"Aye..." he says, smirking as his lips press tight to mine.

DARE

I't's my day of reckoning, that's what it is. I wake earlier than I ought to, naked as the day I was born, with an equally naked American girl clinging to me like I'm the best goddamn teddy bear in the world. Grace breathes softly, her cheek on my chest, a perfect pillow, her hair framing her face like a golden angel gathering her rest after a long day of being absolutely heavenly.

That's what you are, Grace Turner. That's what you'll always be to me. You're perfect. You are heaven.

The sun shines up from its dark corner of the Earth, poking little tempting rays of light through the edges of the curtains in Grace's hotel room. Small shimmers become a radiant glow, lines of light crossing the darkness. One shimmery line crawls from the curtain to the bed and across my pretty little American girl's bare backside, her leg draped across me. I take a peek down at that delicious ass of hers, craning my neck for a better view.

Oi, the things I'd do to smack that bouncy feckin' butt right about now.

She's sleeping, though. There are a few things I know to be always true in this world, and one of them is never go waking a woman who's sound asleep. You risk your life doing so. Aye, it'd mean I spend the rest of my life with her, shortening it as such, but I somewhat hoped I'd last a little longer than just one single night, alright? No point in damning myself this soon.

I'll do it on our honeymoon instead. Perfect, yeah?

When I turn my eyes away from her ass, I find her staring at me, plump lips pursed, eyes narrowed.

"What are you doing?" she asks.

"You want the truth?" I counter.

"Mmff," she murmurs, sleepy, nodding against my chest.

"I was staring at that glorious arse of yours. Look at the curves on you, little lady. You're grabbable and smackable all over, aren't ya?"

"I would have thought you had plenty of time to look at my curves last night!" she says, trying to act indignant, but yawning at the end. "If I'm so grabbable and smackable, why aren't you--"

Listen. There's another thing I know to be true in this world, and it's that if you're given a goddamn golden opportunity, well... you take it. And that's exactly what I do.

I slip away from her sleepy cheek, her head plopping to

the bed below. Sitting up quick, I reach out and grab her ass in my hand, really dig my fingers in, then I rise up and smack her arse, watching her beautiful curves bounce beneath my palm.

Never been more satisfied in my whole entire life, I'll tell you right now.

Grace mumbles, laughing into the bed, then she squirms up and away, launching her petite frame at me, trying to tickle me. I roll away from her, grabbing her sides and tickling her first. She bursts into giddy giggles, screaming bloody murder at me, hands and legs flailing all over the damn place.

"Calm yourself, Grace Turner!" I shout, grinning wide, doing my damnedest to hold back a laugh.

"You can go to Hell, Dare Mackenzie!" she shrieks, kicking up a storm.

"Oi, look at that language!" I say, giving in and laughing this time. "What would your mother think?"

I ease up so she can catch her breath, but all she does with her peace is reach out for my waist to tickle me.

"My mother would think you're a terribly rude Irish bad boy who wouldn't know a good thing if it bit him in the ass!" she shrieks, before falling into a fit of giggles again.

Truth be told, the giggling's my fault. I start tickling her again, because why the hell not?

"Haven't ever been bit in the arse by a good thing yet," I tell her. "You offering?"

"You just turn around and see!" she shrieks.

Well, if that's not a challenge I don't know what is, so...

I let her up, flip myself onto my stomach, and give her free reign.

"Let's see if I can figure this one out," I say, looking over my shoulder at her.

"I'll do it," she says, baring her teeth at me like the cutest vampire you've ever seen in your entire life. "Don't think I won't!"

"Aye, I know you will," I say, winking at her.

Fast, like a little giggly demon, she latches onto my hips with her hands, then puts a good chunk of one cheek between her teeth. She nibbles a little, so I flex a glute, putting on a show for her. She nibbles harder, really enjoying that teeth sinking feeling, then she hops up and smacks my butt.

"Shite," I say, one brow raised, looking back at her. "Did something good just bite me on the arse?"

"Uh huh," she says, nodding fast. "Me!"

"How was it?"

"You've got a nice butt," she says, taking a second to admire it. "Do that flexing thing again?"

"As you wish, love."

Back and forth, I flex my glutes for her. She grins at me, watching, wicked. Her hand stretches out, grabbing my butt, feeling my muscles as I flex.

"As much as I'd love to lay in bed all day with you, I think that'd be trouble," I tell her, flipping around on my back.

And now her hand's opposite my butt, palm pressed against my crotch. She moves her hand lower, cupping my balls, my half-hard morning erection stretching lazily up towards my stomach, a stiff awakening.

"I have to be at the airport by noon," she says, pouting at me.

"Aye, I figured as much," I tell her.

"I wish I didn't."

"Come here," I say, pulling her so she's straddling me.

She comes, knees at my sides, those delicious, athletic thighs of hers resting against mine. Somehow, though I doubt it's altogether coincidental, the lips of her pussy lay perfectly around my half-erect shaft. Not going to be half-erect for long if this keeps up. Honestly I'm not even half-erect a second after she's straddling me; there's a full-on erection where the half used to be.

"I want you inside me again," she says, pressing her palms against my chest.

"Do ya now?" I ask, shifting my hips to the side, sliding down just enough that the head of my cock lines up perfectly with her pussy.

"Dare..." she says, shaking her head at me.

"Aye?" I ask, all angels and innocence.

She pushes down against me, sliding back, my cock slipping inside her, easy like a beautiful Sunday morning.

"I know what you're doing..." she says, more shakes of her head, her light blonde hair swaying back and forth.

"Seems to me you're the one doing it, not me," I point out.

"You're tempting me," she adds. "It's not my fault."

"I'll tempt you every single day of my entire life if you don't stop me."

"Will you?" she asks, sliding back and forth across my core, riding me nice and slow.

"That's a promise, Grace Turner," I say, crossing my heart with my finger. "Us Mackenzie men, we never break our promises, especially when it comes to the women we're going to spend the rest of our lives with."

"You say really sweet words," she says, putting a finger against my lips. "I like sweet words, but what I really like are the actions that back them up. What do you think of that?"

"I think you're going a damn good job with actions right about now," I say, truthful.

"Jerk," she says, laughing. "That's not what I meant!"

"Aye, well, you can't ask me to think properly when you're riding my cock, woman."

"What, this?" she asks, tossing her hair over her shoulder, giving me an innocent look that would impress even the purest of nuns.

Except there's no fooling me, Grace. I can see exactly what you're doing, and you're doing a fantastic job of it, might I add.

"I've always, um... been kind of self-conscious of this," she says, whispering to me. "Doing this. Like this."

"What for, beautiful?"

"I don't know? I mean, is it good? I... I was told once that, um..."

"No need to mince words, love."

"I had a boyfriend once who told me that I wasn't very good. At this. Being on top. And..."

"Well, first off, he's an arse. Second, you're damn good

from my point of view. Amazing view *and* you've some moves on you. But just so we're on the same page, and since I want to make sure you're feeling real confident about your abilities, let me just--"

I grab her hips as she rides me. She doesn't need my help. I'm a minute or less away from filling her up with a sticky good morning. I can't stand the idea that she thinks she's not good enough, though. Pisses me right the fuck off.

"So... aye, fuck, right there. You feel that?" I ask her.

It's right when she, there you go, beautiful. Fuck. Can't even. What was I saying? Aye, right when she slides deep onto my cock and the head starts to swell a little more, pressing in hard.

"Mmm," she says, grinning wide. "I feel that. I like it."

"You keep that up and let's see what happens, yeah?" I say, winking at her.

"Oh? What'll happen?" she asks, coy, pouting those perfect little plump lips of hers.

"Just keep it up, Grace Turner," I say, shaking my head at her. "If you're late for your flight don't blame me, though. If you *are* late, I'm dragging you back to mine and keeping you until you can get another flight, though."

"Promise?" she asks, sliding down my body, arching her back, showing off her delicious curves, and putting on a show.

I grab one of her breasts, then the other. Gotta maintain balance, yeah? I play with her nipples while she practices her riding skills on me.

"Ohhhh," she whispers. "I... I shouldn't have done this..."

"Why's that?" I ask, because from the scrunched up look on her face she doesn't believe any of the words coming out of her mouth.

"Shhh," she says, thrusting her finger against my lips again.

Don't have to tell me twice. I sit back and relax, basking in the glory that is my American girl riding me like there's no tomorrow. I almost forget that there won't be a tomorrow for us, either. I'll be here and she'll be there, but none of that matters right now.

My cock throbs, digging in deep inside her. She rolls her hips, grinding against me, enjoying every flowing sensation. She's a goddamn goddess right now, that's what she is. I sprang that bad girl of hers free and this is what I get. The good girl knows it's alright to let loose every now and then.

A little naughty now and then never hurt anyone.

It's not long before a little naughty becomes a lot of sweating, grunting, moaning, pulsing, and throbbing, the bed bucking beneath our bodies as she slams her hips against mine. I grab her and pull her against me hard, and she fights back, claiming my orgasm as her own. She gives me one hell of an orgasm in return; both hers and mine.

"Fuck, woman," I say, stroking her hair as she lays atop me, completely spent.

"I just did!" she says, laughing at her own joke.

"You can't laugh at your own jokes, love," I say, but I start laughing out loud, too.

"We... I mean, I... or... do you want to go to breakfast with me?" she asks. "In the hotel? It's free?"

"Was that last one a question?"

"Noooo! It is free. It's a nice buffet. Are you hungry? You can eat as much as you want."

"I will never turn down an all-you-can-eat breakfast," I tell her. "Especially with my beautiful American girl."

"Mine," she says, making a show of grabbing me wherever she can. Basically she grabs my arm as it's the easiest part to reach, but I think she'd grab all of me if she weren't so tired. "You're mine."

"We should take a shower first," I say, kissing her cheek. "Can you walk?"

"Can... you carry me?" she asks.

"Is that your way of saying I've done a number on you and your legs and your ability to walk? Shite. How're you going to get to the airport now? I'll have to keep you."

"Shut up!" she says, slapping my chest, sticking her tongue out at me. "I can walk but I would like it if you carried me because it'd be cute and nice, don't you think?"

"You think so?" I ask, grabbing her butt tight.

"Mhm!"

I steel myself, sitting up with her, holding her arse in my hands. She wraps her legs around my waist as we shimmy to the side of the bed, and then I bounce up and off to a stand. She clings to me like warm sunshine on a bright summer's day while I carry her to the bathroom. Reaching out, she switches on the lights, then pushes the door shut behind us as I make our way to the glass-walled shower stall in the corner.

Grace Turner, if I had all day with you, we'd be stuck in this shower for at least an hour. You're damn lucky you've got a plane to catch. And I'm damn lucky I get to soak your body down with soap and suds and run my hands across every inch of you in the name of cleaning up for breakfast.

Maybe we're even now. Squared up.

Maybe.

GRACE

Showered, dressed, and supposedly ready for the day, Dare and I walk down the hall towards the breakfast lounge. The shower was... let's call it interesting. Interesting in the fact that I don't think either of us wanted to leave the comfort of hot steam and water, glass walls surrounding us, but as everything falls into place, reality sets in, too.

I tap my keycard against the electronic lock on the right side of the frosted glass doors and they slide apart, ushering us into the lounge. Dare stands at my side, peeking left and right, curious, before I laugh at him and hop through the entryway to go get my breakfast.

"My American girl's a fancy one, eh?" he says, grinning at me as I leave him behind to march my way right up to the buffet stand.

"You keep saying that! It's not that fancy, is it?" I ask, looking all around.

"Aye, most would call this fancy, Grace."

"Well, *I'm* not that fancy, so you're just going to have to deal with it."

"I'll *deal* with you alright," he says, coming up to my side, whispering a growl in my ear.

"I think you did that *plenty* last night and then this morning, too," I tell him, leaning over quick to kiss his cheek. "Now, be good and eat breakfast with me."

I bend down and grab a plate from a shelf below the buffet stand. We're the only ones in line now, so we get prime pick of everything on offer. I start at one end, filling my plate with scrambled eggs, a few crispy fried hashbrowns, two sausages, however many pieces of bacon I haphazardly grab with the tongs they have available, and...

Dare Mackenzie stares at me like I've got five heads. But he's filling up his own plate just the same, so I don't know what this boy is looking at me funny for!

"Hungry?" he asks, smirking.

"You shush your mouth and let me pick my food in peace," I tell him.

Which I do. I add a cute little pecan pastry to the side of my plate, and I top everything off with a tiny porcelain cup of bircher muesli that I slip into the only remaining spot on my plate next to my scrambled eggs.

There! Perfect.

While Dare finishes gathering his own grub, I scoot away to find us a table. The breakfast lounge is a mix of posh looking loveseats fitted against the walls with square tables in front of them, high stools tucked in spots with less real estate with small hightop circle tablestands between them, and some larger oval tables scattered throughout the center with four or more chairs circling those.

I duck and dodge around the people already seated and go to my favorite spot. I sat alone last time, but this time I'll have company to enjoy the view with. Thankfully the seats are empty, probably because the table is tiny, barely big enough for two people unless they like being cozy together.

And... well, I do. I like being cozy with Dare. I like it very much.

Dare glances around, confused at all the decorations. It's easy to tell he's used to a more quaint Irish pub setting. I kind of like being able to show him this side of my trip even if I don't usually stay at places like this.

"That's a right feast you've made yourself," he says, teasing, sitting opposite me on the other high stool.

"I need to eat!" I tell him. "I do a lot, you know? I'm on the volleyball team and I barely have time to eat in between practice and going to rehearsals at drama club. And I have homework to do after that. Do you know how hard it is to eat healthy when you're doing so much?"

"Aye, so you eat as much as you can when you can," he says, that endless grin stuck on his face.

"If you don't start being good I'll poke at your plate, too. Meanie."

To put some bite into my threat, I snatch a piece of bacon from his plate. Ha! And I munch it in front of him. Dare gapes at me like I've stolen his one and only piece of bacon, and what a horrible person I must be for having done it. But then he just steals one of my pieces from my plate and chomps down on it.

"What a thief," I say, shaking my head.

"Takes one to know one, Grace Turner," he says, grinning wide at me.

A woman comes over while we're staring at each other, forgetting to eat. She looks intrigued and confused, like she's never seen a pair like us before.

"Can I get you two some coffee?" she asks.

"I'll have a mocha, please," I say, chipper and cute.

Dare groans and shakes his head at me before turning back to the girl, "Can I get a black coffee? Thanks, love."

The waitress beams and shuffles off to get our cups.

I scrunch up my brow and pout my lips, staring at this Irish ruffian across from me. He digs into his scrambled eggs before noticing me eyeballing him.

"What?" he asks, half talking, half chewing.

"Do you just call everyone love?" I ask.

"Nah, wouldn't call a guy it," he says, shaking his head. "Would've gone with 'mate' then."

"What about when you call me love?"

"Well, it's a different kind of love, isn't it?"

"Is it?"

"Aye, love, it is," he says, teasing me. "See? Just did it."

"Well, mate, I'm not sure I see it."

"You'll need to practice saying your mates more, Grace.

That one's alright, but... if I'm being truthful, it could use some work."

"I'll *mate* you!" I... say... without thinking of any of those words in that combination... or what else they could mean.

At which point the woman who went to get our coffee comes back. She blushes, cheeks as bright as sunrise, puts our coffee cups down between us, and shuffles off fast.

"Will you now?" Dare asks, winking. "That a promise, love?"

"I'm not talking to you ever again. I'm eating my breakfast now. Mmff!"

That last mumble is the sound of me eating my breakfast. That's what it's supposed to be. Also, I need some sound to distract me from how hot my cheeks feel right now.

I'll mate you... really now, Grace. Ugh.

My silence only lasts for a few seconds, maybe a minute at most. Dare and I talk about this and that, volleyball, my college, his future plans, my possible plans, what I'm going to do when I get back, so on and so forth. It's nice, but then I interrupt him quick because it's about to happen.

"What's about to happen?" he asks.

"Shhh!" I say, holding a finger to my lips.

A man dressed in a three-piece suit comes out from one of the serving corridors. He walks to a spot at the end of the room, reaches for the rope pulley near the edge of the curtains that flow all along this side of the breakfast lounge, and starts tugging, pulling the curtains back. Foot by foot, the curtain at one side slowly starts peeling away, revealing the floor to ceiling glass wall next to us.

As our section of curtain pulls away, the secret garden Dare and I passed through last night pops into view. This time during the morning, though. The sun shimmers up just above the trimmed hedges at the end of the garden, light shining onto the garden proper. Morning dew glistens on grass and luminous sparkles of watercover glimmer on the wrought-iron tables and chairs set through the garden. It's still early spring, so there aren't as many colorful flowers as they likely have during full summer, but evergreen shrubs line the future flower patches, pristinely trimmed into different shapes. Pure white marble platforms and statues accent different sections of the garden, white becoming even whiter with the new glow of the morning sun.

"Breathtakingly beautiful," Dare says.

I stare out into the gardens, admiring and enjoying the view of my last morning here. "Isn't it?"

"The garden's lovely, aye, but I was talking about your smile and the way your face lights up when you look at it."

I stumble on my thoughts, cheeks blushing bright. Glancing away from the gardens for a second, I peek over at him and see him smiling at me, genuine, love and joy in his eyes.

"Let's finish our breakfast," Dare says, never taking his eyes off me. "I've something to tell you, Grace Turner."

DARE

"**L**et's go see this secret garden of yours," I say to Grace once we're finished up with our breakfast, empty plates and scraps of food sitting cold between the two of us.

"Alright," she says with an anxious smile.

Aye, that's about the way I feel right now, too. Maybe not anxious so much as wondering what it is between us that's gotten me so riled up over the past twenty-four hours. Hasn't even been that long and here I am thinking about what it'd be like if I had a million more years with my beautiful American girl.

If my mum could see me now, she'd call me a fool. You're a damn fool, Dare Mackenzie. How could you put that poor American girl through all that. Don't you know any better? I thought I knocked some sense into that thick head of yours when you were a wee lad, but here you are acting an idiot, not even saying the things you know you should be saying.

Oi, mum, calm yourself.

Aye, I'll have that conversation later, I'm sure. For now, I'm gonna have one that's a bit harder than that. Just a bit. Don't mind me and my fool self.

I take Grace's hand in mine as we head to a deck door off to the side of the breakfast lounge. Opening it for the pretty lady, I never let go of her hand, keeping it tight where it belongs, right inside mine. We step out into the brisk spring air, chiller than either of us came prepared for.

Makes no matter. I won't keep her long. We've both got business going on today.

"What's wrong?" she asks, turning to me as we head out into the garden proper.

I spot a little stone white archway in the distance, guiding us towards it. We step through, Grace eyeing me like a kitten just brought to the vet, not knowing what's going on, where they are, or why the person they trusted so much is bringing them to this strange, unknown place with such bright lights and strangeness all around.

Turns out we're in a hedge maze of sorts, but that's not the reason Grace Turner's giving me eyes as such.

"Aye, well, nothing's wrong," I say, stepping along the path, one shuffled step at a time. That's how I need to do this. Just one step, then another, on like that. "It's only... I've got a secret. One I'd've loved to tell you before, but now that we've spent the night together and I know you better I want to do it proper. At the right time and in the right place. Now's neither of those."

She flickers her pretty little lashes at me, batting heavy with a bit of confusion and uncertainty, but a wee ounce of trust glimmering in those round baby blues.

"When?" she asks.

A simple question, but what's the right answer?

"Do you trust me?" I ask her.

She flashes me a worried, yet silly smirk. "You're not married are you? Dating someone? Promised? What's going on?"

"Nah, not yet. We can fix that right quick, though," I say, giving her a grin to ease her worries as best I can. "Will you marry me, Grace Turner?"

"You didn't even get on one knee!" she says, rolling her eyes and laughing at me.

"You American girls sure are finicky, aren't ya?"

"And how would you know, Dare Mackenzie?" she counters. "You've only met one."

"Aye, and this one sure is finicky."

She rolls her eyes even more, throwing me an extra exaggerated groan to go with it.

Holding her hand tight in mine, I get to one knee and look up at her.

"Shut up," she says, standing, legs quivering. "Get up, you! You... you can't just..."

"Aye, well, I'm doing this the way I want to do it," I tell her. "Listen, I'm asking you something, Grace Turner. I won't ask you to marry me. Not now. Not again, either. You keep turning me down, woman. Oi. You're doing a number on my ego, you know that?"

"Oh, right. I'm sure you're so terribly hurt," she says. Her eyes can't even roll hard enough; her entire head's in on the game now.

I grin, winking up at her, but then getting back to the serious parts. "I'll tell you the secret next Friday. Can you hold off until then?"

"I... I think so?" she says, looking down at me, at our hands clenched together tight like neither of us ever wants to let go even if we know we've got to soon. "Um, how? Can we talk between then? I..."

"Aye," I tell her. "Message me on WhatsApp. Or friend me on Facebook. Or both. I'll gladly take as many ways to talk to you as I can. Might even give you a ring one evening if you're lucky. Not quite the same as the one you're asking after now. Wedding ring'll come later, love."

She scrunches up her face and sticks her tongue out at me. I want to kiss it, and lick her, and do all sorts of cute, inappropriate, adorably deviant things to, with, and for her.

Grace Turner is beautiful chaos incarnate and I can't take my eyes off of her. Don't think I can keep any part of myself away from her. I wanted to try hard, wanted to keep this simple and straightforward, but I've never been great at following rules, especially the ones I make for myself when I know they make no sense.

I want to go back to bed with her, bring her to dinner at my parent's house, make love to her underneath the stars in the Irish countryside, sit and read books with her for hours, screw her ever-loving brains out, be young and dumb, grow old and grey, and be with her every other which way thing you can think of.

"You won't forget to tell me the secret, will you?" she asks.

And with her eyes, she asks another question. *I won't forget her, will I?*

"There's no possible way I would ever forget anything having to do with you, Grace Turner," I say to her.

GRACE

(Almost a week later.)

I never told anyone what happened last weekend. It still seems so strange and confusing to me. Did I really go to Ireland out of the blue like that? No, not out of the blue. I spent months planning for it, but... I think a small part of me always thought I'd chicken out at the last minute. It's one thing to do something spontaneously, but it's another to do it both planned and spur of the moment.

I always thought I could have just... not went, you know? Canceled my plane ticket, called the hotel and asked for a refund on my reservation. I don't know what would have happened then. I never really thought about it until the last second and at the last second I figured, hey, why not?

Why not indeed!

The obvious reason for "why not" is that people have been

incredibly suspicious of me checking my phone every time it beeps, my newfound appreciation for sneaking away quickly to send text messages to some mysterious person that I refuse to name, my unusual fascination with WhatsApp, and my sudden bouts of smiles that tend to overtake me soon after these enigmatic messages.

The latter's especially complicated because of the play we're putting on in drama club next month. I'm standing on stage after a quick break, smiling my arse off as that awful Dare Mackenzie would probably say, and I'm supposed to be weeping mournfully and driving into a monologue about my dearly departed husband and how life will just never be the same ever again.

Sorry, fictional husband. It's hard not to grin like an idiot when Dare sends me subtly sexy pictures of him having just stepped out of a shower as he texts me to tell me that he'll be sure to think of me long and hard, over and over again, as he starts his day. And, you know, the silly witty banter. The jokes. Ugh. Why is he so charming? I can't get his accent out of my head, either. It's like nothing even sounds the same anymore. Except everything does sound the same. It's the exact same sounds that I've always heard.

I hate that Irish accents are sexy. And I hate that Dare has a wonderful one. And I especially hate how he can tease me about everything but it sounds stupidly attractive and loving and like he's being an asshole all at the same time.

Hate hate hate it, except I love it so much, too.

Dare Mackenzie, you're an absolute jerk and you're going to haunt me for the rest of my life, I know it.

Except he hasn't. Not today. The last text I received from him was this morning when he asked me if I remembered his promise.

To which I immediately texted back:

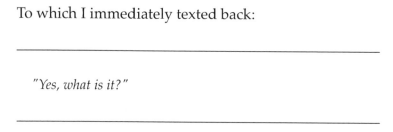

"Yes, what is it?"

Because, you know, he told me he'd tell me something today, right? Yup, I distinctly remember that, so...

Nothing. Not a peep during my classes earlier this morning. I tried to be patient, waited to see the telltale little WhatsApp checkmarks turn to blue saying he read my last message. Sometime during lunch they switched from gray to blue. That's the last time he was online. I've checked nearly every hour since then and... nothing. Not online. No reply.

Dare Mackenzie is nowhere to be found. He's missing.

I miss him so much...

I don't know what any of this means. It was just a whirlwind weekend romance, that's what it was. It's bound to die off, right? Please ignore the fact that we've texted every night, called each other to talk a couple times, and even if neither of us has said it I feel like we're dating now. He's basically my boyfriend. I think. Does he think I'm his girlfriend? I... I mean, I think so...?

Yes, I have a mysterious secret boyfriend after going on a trip I never told anyone about, and I know exactly how that sounds which is probably why I am definitely one-hundred percent absolutely never going to tell anyone.

That's the plan, sort of. We'll see how it goes.

"Grace!" Amanda shouts at me as I miss an easy toss from the other side of the net.

Volleyball practice. Yes. My mind isn't anywhere close to the court at the moment. I glance over at the ball as it bounces once more and thuds to a halt to my left, just outside the lines in the gym. I'm sure it was inside the lines when I completely missed it soaring past my head, but that doesn't help me much right now.

"Sorry!" I say, wincing, eyebrows scrunched up, bottom lip finding a home tucked between my teeth.

"Guys, let's take a quick water break," Sandy, our team captain, says. She's amazing, and I love how supportive she is, but I also know I'm about to get a gentle verbal thrashing once we're on the sidelines.

I go to chug down some water quick first, hopping next to my translucent pink water bottle that *coincidentally* has my phone laying next to it. I mean, most of the girls keep their phones out on the sidelines during practice, but no one goes to check them much. Except during breaks.

Now's a break, right?

No! I... I need some self control. Will power. You can do this, Grace. I believe in you. Which is me. I believe in myself.

This is all going great and wonderful and excellent, but then my phone beeps, the screen lights up, and a notification flashes quickly.

"New Message from Dare Mackenzie."

Sandy's coming. I need that. I need to get my head back in the game. And I will. I promise. I won't let some Irish bad boy stop me from doing amazing things. I'm the star volleyball player, lead female in all the school plays, and I have one of the highest GPAs to boot, which is definitely important for my future.

I'm stuck in the past right now, though.

I really loved that one weekend where I got to forget everything and be a girl who didn't have to act responsible all the time, could go a little wild and be a little free, and who accidentally fell in love with a boy who told her she was his everything.

I unlock my phone, open up WhatsApp, and check the message. It's not a text one, but one of those fancy voice ones. I tap the play button quick and hold the phone up to my ear, listening. It's only a few seconds long but in my experience sometimes the briefest things are the ones that are the most incredibly powerful and intense.

"Afternoon, beautiful. I don't want to distract you too much while you're busy, but if you get a chance you should turn around right quick, love. Will only take a second."

Um, what?

Sandy looks at me for a fraction of a second as our eyes lock, but then she glances behind me over my shoulder. Something changes, her eyes lighting up like she's suddenly realized... *something*. I don't know what yet. It's so strange watching it happen like this, but I immediately know the *something* has to do with me.

Don't ask me how, or why, or what makes me feel that way, but...

I turn around. Right quick, as they say.

Standing there, walking towards me with a slow and steady gait, only a few yards away now, is the man of my dreams. And he's a complete jerk. An absolute asshole! What the hell is he doing here? He made me wait all day for a reply and now he's... he's here...

"You..." I say, staring at him.

"Aye, it's me," he says, cocking a grin my way. "Seems it's you, too, yeah?"

"You're an asshole," I say, trying not to laugh or cry and probably failing at both.

"True on all accounts, Grace Turner," he says, holding out his hands. "Can I get a hug, love?"

"What are you even doing here!" I half shout, half whisper. I know those aren't even close to the same, but my mind's all mixed up right now, and...

I run at him, leap into his arms, wrap my arms tight around him, holding him as close as I can. He slowly winds his arms around me, holding me close, embracing me for everything I am, all the beauty and love and fun and wonder of our weekend together coming back in that simple hug.

"I missed you, Grace," he whispers into my ear. "You've no idea how hard it was to keep this a secret."

"How are you here?" I ask, but before he can answer I kiss him.

This isn't some romance movie kiss. We aren't locking lips. No one's cheering. I'm pressing my lips to every last inch of his face, all of it, everywhere I can. His nose, cheeks, forehead, eyes, sometimes his lips. I don't care what I'm kissing, I just want to kiss all of him.

He laughs and squirms but I cling to him. He doesn't even try to free himself from me. He just lets me kiss him every which way, all over, over and over again.

I know I said this wasn't some romance movie kiss before, but, um... we've attracted a crowd. Literally all of the girls from the volleyball team stand around us in a circle, gushing, intrigued and curious as to what's going on and who this Irish stud is.

"So this is your distraction?" Sandy asks, grinning from ear to ear. "He's a cute one."

"Aye, I do my best," Dare says, grinning back. "You're taking care of my American girl, I take it?"

"Um, we're all American girls," I remind him. "You're in the US now."

"Shite, do I need a new pet name for you?" he asks.

"Well, he did say *my* American girl," Amanda points out. "That's different than just saying an American girl."

I think my cheeks suddenly realize what a big volleyball team we have because they decide now is an opportune moment to burn bright red in severe embarrassment.

My American Girl.

It was different in Ireland. It's not like there were as many American girls around. Now, though, um...

We're surrounded by them, but I'm still his. Nothing's changed. I think I like it even more now, actually.

"So, um... girls... this is Dare. Dare Mackenzie. He's absolutely awful, but he's pretty cute and I like him. He's from Ireland."

Which gets a collective *ooh* and *aah* from everyone.

"An exchange student?" one of my teammates, Alice, asks. "When did you meet him? He must have gotten here recently. I don't think I've seen him around."

"Got here a couple hours ago," Dare says with a nod.

"Ummm," Amanda mumbles, pursing her lips for a second. "So... you two met a couple of hours ago?"

"Not exactly?" I say, shifty-eyed.

"Oi, you're keeping me a secret, are ya?" Dare asks, smirking at me.

"I wasn't keeping you a secret!" I say, pouting at him. "I..."

"She was *definitely* keeping you a secret," Sandy says. "Our Gracie's been missing easy tosses, glancing over at her phone every other minute, laughing at random text messages in the locker room, and all sorts of other boy crazy behavior. I guess I can see why now, though. Hmm."

The other girls nod, appreciating my hunk of man meat over here. Dare smirks, taking it all in, but then he smiles at me and me alone, hugging me tight.

"I... may have accidentally ended up in Ireland last weekend and Dare rescued me from falling into the river."

"Aye, I feckin' knew you'd admit it one of these days!" he says, excitedly proclaiming his victory. "Didn't think you'd do it so quick, but I'm glad we got that one over with, love."

"You... were in *Ireland*... last weekend..." Sandy says, crossing her arms over her chest, glaring me down.

"I swear you told me you were going back home," Melanie says, tilting her head to the side. "You live in Ireland, Grace?"

"Ummm... so.. it's a long story?" I say.

Curse you and your sexy Irish accent and making me tell all the girls exactly what happened. Curse you a billion times, Dare Mackenzie!

P.S. I love you.

"Spill it," Sandy says. "Long break, girls. Grace is going to tell us a story. Dare, you can stay. Make sure she tells the truth."

"Aye, of course," he says, tilting his head into a nod. "You can count on me."

"Jerk," I mutter, hugging him one last time before pulling away to explain the whole thing to my team.

GRACE

"And then I said, 'Grace Turner, I can't kiss you yet. I want to get to know you better first,' and she looked me straight in the eyes with those beautiful baby blues of hers, that cute little pout on her lips, and I tried my best but I couldn't help it anymore, so I--"

Dare's rendition of our weekend together is not entirely accurate, if you couldn't tell.

"Um, excuse me, wasn't *I* supposed to be telling this story?" I ask him.

"Aye, I thought I'd help you out a bit," he says, grinning at me.

"Well, you're not helping, because none of that happened!"

The girls on my volleyball team collectively sigh, dreamy and wistful, mostly ignoring the fact that, nope, none of that happened!

I mean, alright, so we *did* stare into each other's eyes a

time or two. And we *did* have a talk about who was or wasn't kissing the other or what that involved and Dare *may* have told me that he really wanted to kiss me at one point or another, but still!

"Near the end, I could tell I was close," Dare continues, brushing off my protest from before. "It was written in the stars and I saw a lot of those that night while we were walking back to her place. I didn't want to presume anything, but I needed to make my intentions clear, so I got down on one knee and I asked my beautiful American girl for her hand in marriage."

"What did she say?" Sandy asks, wide-eyed, completely caught up in his tale.

"Oh, yes, what did I say?" I ask Dare, rolling my eyes.

He winks at me quick then goes back to telling our story. "Well, ladies, that's why I'm here. Wanted to make sure to properly introduce myself as Grace's future husband. Not sure if she's taking my name or not, but Grace Mackenzie's got a nice ring to it, yeah?"

"Speaking of rings..." I say, shaking my head and looking down at my obviously ringless finger.

"You took it off!" Dare says, acting shocked.

"You never gave me one!" I say right back at him.

"Well, you should've asked for one, now shouldn't ya?"

"I did ask!" I say, laughing. "Ugh. You're the worst. The absolute worst."

"Oi, does that mean the wedding's off?" he asks, tossing another one of his mischievous, emerald-eyed winks at me.

"I didn't say that..." I say.

"You heard her, ladies. The wedding's still on. You're all invited, of course. It'll be grand. Where're we having her, Grace? The Irish countryside might be nice, but I know you American girls are big on weddings in churches, yeah?"

"I didn't agree to marry you, either!" I counter. "You're awful. You're too much, Dare Mackenzie. Calm yourself. Down boy."

"Oi. Yes'm," he says, polite as a raccoon that's just stolen a fish and is running off with it.

"There's one part of the story that you missed, though," I remind him.

"Yeah?"

And it's something I desperately need to know. It's nice that he's here. I don't want to sound like I'm complaining about that. It's just...

"Why are you here now?" I ask him. "How did you find me?"

"Aye, well... that's the secret, innit? The promise I made to you. When we were talking on St. Paddy's Day in the pub, at some point a thing or two clicked in my mind. I wouldn't've walked you back to your room if I knew nothing could come of us, Grace. I surely would've loved to, but... I wouldn't've wanted to break either of our hearts like that, either. You brought up your uni a time or two and I put two and two together, so... surprise! I'm coming here for a semester abroad as an exchange student."

"Um, excuse me?"

"I think he said--" Melanie starts to say, the other girls nodding all around us.

"No, um, I heard that, but... you're here for the whole semester? What semester? The semester's almost over and then there's summer break, and--"

"Aye, well, figured I'd get here early so I could enjoy some of your American summer. I hear you've some nice beaches. Couldn't hurt to get a head start on the next year, either."

"And you planned all of this... when?"

"Would you believe me if I told you it was in the works before we even met?" he asks, smiling wide.

"Not particularly!" I say, sticking my tongue out at him.

"Aye, well, 'twas. Which is why you've got to marry me now, Grace Turner. It's fate. We were destined to meet. I can't deny something so strong. Are ya gonna marry me yet or do I have to keep asking?"

"You haven't even gotten me a ring!" I say, laughing, smiling, and maybe crying a little. Happy tears, though. Silly, excited, happy tears.

Suddenly someone slams the gym doors open, standing between the pair of them with tousled hair and a glow of mad exertion on her face like she's been running all around looking for something... or someone...

Which she soon finds standing in the center of the ring of girls from the volleyball team.

"Dare!" she shouts out. "Ugh. You ran off when I was trying to check you into the dorms to show you around. You can't just--"

"Brittany!" Dare says, grinning and waving at her. "Have ya met my wife? Grace, this is Brittany. She's my cousin.

Cheerleader type, yeah? Pom poms or somewhat? Brittany, do ya have pom poms still?"

"Yes, I do," the head cheerleader says. "Wait, what? You're married? To Grace?"

"Um, hi, Brittany," I say, sheepish, holding up my hand the tiniest amount, barely waving.

"Dare, you can't just go marrying Grace," Brittany says.

"Aye, that's what she keeps telling me," Dare says.

"He hasn't even given me a ring," I add with a nod.

"I've got to get her a ring. You American girls are finicky like that."

"You can't just... it doesn't work like that!" Brittany says, stomping her foot.

"Brittany's gonna want to come to the wedding," Dare says, turning to me. "Family and all. Hope you don't mind. You two know each other?"

"Well, that'd be nice," I say. "We're friends and all, so..."

"We can talk about this later," Brittany says, stomping up to Dare and grabbing his ear. "Oh, cousin of mine, stop seducing the star volleyball player your first day here and let me finish showing you around, dammit!"

"Seduced her before I even got here," Dare says, winking as Brittany drags him off.

"Wait, um... what?"

"He was just telling us the story," Sandy adds. "It's so dreamy, Brittany!"

"I'll introduce you lasses to some fine Irish gentleman I know back home if you'd like," Dare adds.

"No," Brittany says. "Don't even start with me. I know

what your friends are like. Ugh. Grace! You, too. Come! We're going to get to the bottom of this."

I mean, what am I supposed to say to that? I shrug to my teammates, mouthing the word "sorry" to them as I jog off to follow Brittany and Dare out of the gym.

"It's fine," Sandy says, to me and the rest of the girls. "Let's pack up and get some rest so we can come at this fresh tomorrow. It'll be better that way. Good work today, girls!"

And... that's how I meet my new cousin-in-law?

I knew her before, but I don't know if that's important.

Wait! I didn't even agree to marry my awful Irish bad boy scoundrel yet, either. He's much too mischievous. He didn't even swim the Atlantic for me. I bet he flew here. On a plane! The nerve. Ugh.

I love Dare so much it hurts.

DARE

"Look, Grace," my cousin says to her. "You really can't go around seducing my cousin when you take completely spur of the moment, uncharacteristic trips like that. I thought you were the responsible one here."

"What!" Grace says, gasping out the word. "Brittany, I just told you what happened, and I don't think anywhere in there did I mention that I seduced Dare. And maybe the trip was a little irresponsible but I... I just, um... I needed some time, you know? To myself. To..."

"To seduce my cousin," Brittany says with a nod. "Yeah, I got that part."

"I did no such thing!"

"Aye, well, I do distinctly recall being seduced," I say, butting in. "I remember it like it was last weekend. Fond memories, those."

"You be quiet, Dare Mackenzie!" Grace spouts at me, trying not to laugh.

"I might've involved myself in a bit of the old seduction game, as well. Can't ever be too sure on St. Paddy's Day, yeah?"

"You're both awful," Brittany says, shooing us away with a wave of her hands. "I can't even believe this, Grace! Ugh! I expected as much from Dare, but... you? Come on now..."

"Well, he's very charming when he wants to be," Grace tells her.

As the two girls look at me to size up my charm, I strike a pose, do a bit of eyelash batting, a flex here and there. I'm a good ol' peacock when the mood fits, aye.

"Strictly reserving my charm for my wife now, though," I remind them both.

"You shut your mouth, Dare Mackenzie!" Brittany says, laughing and shoving me away. "You can't go getting married your first week in the US. Auntie will murder me if I let that happen. I'm supposed to keep an eye on you, remember?"

"How about you and Grace trade off on that one?" I offer. "Grace, you'll keep watch of me, yeah? Day and night if you're up for it. Might need extra watch when I'm in bed, though. I'll keep you real close, don't you worry."

"Oh, I'm sure you'd *love* that," Grace says, rolling her eyes.

"Yeah, and, speaking of, I don't think your roommate's going to appreciate that. He's got enough issues as it is, Dare. He's my friend, so I want you to actually try and get along with him, alright?"

"*Friend*, is it?" I ask, lifting one brow, dubious.

"Friend," Brittany repeats herself, stern and steady. "F R I E N D. He has... an I don't know what. I don't know anything. Everyone just does things around here and I can't keep track. At any rate, we're here."

My dear old cousin Brittany dragged me back to the dorms with Grace in hot pursuit. Grace is hot all the time, and I can't say I mind her being in pursuit of me, so it works for me. While we walked our way back to the dorm building, Grace told her the story of how we met. I like my version a wee bit better, but Grace tells it so nicely and I think her version's better suited for family. Safer. Less risk of me saying something I ought not to.

And... well, that's how we got here. To the dorms. Taking a lift to my new dorm room floor. Calling it an elevator. Miscounting the floors as Americans like to do. I won't judge, though. It's interesting and different, just like my future wife-to-be. If Brittany weren't here, I'm sure Grace and I would've enjoyed the lift a lot more. There's a lot of fun times to be had when you're with the girl you love in a lift, let me tell you.

Might tell you later once I'm in the situation. We'll see how that one goes.

Brittany leads us down the hall to one of the doors, then knocks as if we might intrude upon something.

"Is that how it is?" I ask, staring at the door, confused. "Americans knock on doors even when they belong there?"

"Shush, you," Brittany says, tossing me an evil-eyed glare.

"Shhh," Grace says, holding her finger to my lips. "Be good."

I kiss her finger for good luck and she blushes a delicious

shade of apple red. Oi, I love her even more with every passing second.

"You've been the only thing I've thought of for a week," I say, thinking out loud.

Apple red cheeks add a candy red coating on top, reds upon reds. Grace Turner, one day you'll be the death of me. Your beauty knows no bounds.

"I don't think he's here," Brittany says, trying the knob, pushing the door open when she finds it unlocked. "Here, um... go in, I guess."

Gentlemanly, I let Grace in first, then follow behind her, Brittany coming up last.

"That's your--dammit, Scarlet!" my cousin shouts out after pointing towards a bed tucked away in the corner.

The bed's alright. A bed's a bed, good for sleeping and... things best not discussed in front of my cousin. Grace and I'll have an intimate conversation about the finer points of beds at some point, I imagine. The thing is, uh...

"Nothing against it, but purple's not quite my color, and I think I could do without the fluffy wide-eyed animals on that blanket, yeah?"

"What about the pink sheet?" Grace points out, a hint of it poking up at the top of the bed. "I think it fits you."

Oi, my American girl's got jokes, does she.

"Look, the... the bed's not supposed to be like this. I'll take care of it. I'll take care of it right now, actually. If you could just, um... take the comforter and sheets off and act like you never saw them, that'd be nice. Don't tell anyone! Ugh. Seriously, the people around here..."

"Gotcha," I say with a nod. "Mum's the word."

"I have no idea what's going on but I can keep quiet, too," Grace adds.

"If Caleb shows up, just introduce yourself. He knows you're coming. He's probably at football practice right now. I'm sure you two will get along. Caleb's easygoing and nice and fun and... just watch out for Scarlet. She's short but kind of feisty, so don't let her size fool you. Um... I'll leave you two for now, but... don't do anything, please!"

"Gonna just stand here and not move," I say. "Don't even worry about it, cousin."

"Shut up. That's not what I meant," Brittany says, shifty-eyed, looking between me and Grace. "I stuffed your bags in my room when you vanished on me. Grace can show you where it is whenever you're ready. I, um... I'm going to leave you two to talk, alright? Talk! That's it! No... nothing. I don't know. You're both pretty cute together so far, but don't go getting ideas. I don't accept any of this."

And then my dear old cousin leaves, backing away from us slowly, closing the door behind her as she goes.

"Grace Turner, I've got so many ideas right now," I tell her.

"Dare Mackenzie, I've got more than a few ideas, myself..." she says, a little bit of that bad girl glimmer shining in her bright blue eyes.

DARE

"I think we were supposed to be taking the bedding off the bed," she says, bordering on breathless, hurriedly putting her clothes back on.

"Not our fault someone put their bedstuff on my bed," I counter, pulling my pants up and rebuttoning and zipping them.

"You're a terrible influence," she reminds me, as if I didn't already know it.

"You're the one who so very easily let me strip you naked right as soon as we were in a room alone together," I remind her.

"Oh, of course. So easy! It's *all* my fault."

"I wouldn't say *all* your fault. I helped."

Wink, wink, grin.

Grace pushes me playfully, then grabs me in a hug. "I

liked that, but... we need to talk, too. And we can't go having sex all the time, either. I have to keep to my schedule now that I'm back at school and I'm sure you'll have things you need to do, too, so..."

"Aye, we need to talk," I tell her. "I've got some demands of my own, Grace Turner. Why don't you sit your sexy little arse down on my bed and we'll have a discussion of a lifetime."

"A lifetime, eh?" she asks, tilting her head to the side, cute as a button.

Fuck me, woman. Don't go acting a bad girl and immediately start being cute and feckin' adorable after. My cock can only take so much.

Nah, that's not true. I've plenty more to give her and won't be running out of steam any time soon.

I'll let you know how that goes after a few months, but for now I'm good.

"Grace Turner, here are my demands," I say, sitting down, patting a seat next to me.

My lovely little American girl ignores the seat next to me and sits straight in my lap, instead. Grinds down a little, too. Distraction tactics. I know your game, love. I'm on to you.

"Yes?" she asks, batting her lashes at me.

"I want to court you," I tell her.

"Court?" she asks.

"Aye, it's a fancy way of saying I want to go on dates. Boyfriend and girlfriend material. Snog in the corner of some pubs. Fuck our brains out every now and then. You know the deal."

"Well, we're not going into any pubs, because unlike your country we're not allowed in them here. And as for fucking our brains out, um... we both have roommates, so..."

"We're gonna figure that one out," I tell her. "I've some thoughts on the matter and I'll be discussing them with this Caleb fellow once he shows up. If all else fails I'm sure we can find a place or two. Weekends, yeah? And..."

"And...?" she asks after I give her a long pause.

"Do you like movies, Grace? Flicks?"

"I do," she says, smiling at me. "Do you?"

"Aye. Would you like to go to one with me tonight?"

"Tonight?" she says, pursing her lips in thought. "I need to finish some homework--"

"Shite, this is harder than I thought."

"--first," she finishes. "I need to finish some homework *first*, but how about after?"

"And dinner, too," I add. "I want to treat you. My way of hoping you'll forgive me for keeping this exchange student business a secret from you."

"It's a nice secret, though," she says, wrapping her arm around my shoulder and kissing me on the cheek. "I honestly didn't know what to expect at first, and then when I saw you in the gym after you texted me I just kind of froze, but... you're here. You're actually here."

"Aye, I'm here," I say, leaning in and pressing my lips to hers in a soft kiss.

"That doesn't mean this is going to be easy," she points out.

"Never thought it'd be easy," I say, grinning at her. "Don't go making it harder than it ought to be, though."

"I'm just saying..." she says.

"Aye, and I'm saying that I've fallen for you, Grace Turner. Yeah, I can go about wrecking myself over it, thinking about it more than's needed, and worrying over every which way and what for, but... let's just have one argument over it and then be done with it, alright?"

"Sure," she says. "When?"

"After the movie," I say, a quick nod. "We can go get ice cream and argue."

"Taking me out for dinner, a movie, *and* ice cream?" she says, lifting a cute little brow. "You're trying very hard to seduce me, aren't you?"

"Shite, you're on to me," I say, flashing a smirk. "I told you, woman. If we kissed I'd fall in love with you, and I keep my word, I never take it back, and ever since then we've done a whole lot more that's made me fall again and again. I hope we're falling together, Grace. Don't make me fall alone."

"You're not falling alone," she whispers, nuzzling close to me.

"I'm going to get you a ring," I tell her, watching her reaction.

Like I expected, her eyes widen, a brief flit of curiously intrigued nervousness shining in their depths.

"In a few years," I add, sneaking in a kiss to her cheek. "Once we're settled on how nice we are together. I want to take my time with you, Grace Turner. We've got our whole lives, so let's enjoy it, yeah?"

"Yes, please," she says, her voice soft and sweet. "There's so much I want to know about you. I feel like I know a lot, but then there's this other side that I'm only just finding out, and it's like... huh!"

"Aye, like what?" I ask. "What's the first question on your mind?"

"Um, like Brittany's your cousin?"

"I would've told you but I didn't know you knew her. Strange thing to mention in passing."

She giggles, hugging me tight. "True. She's one of my best friends now. She's in the room right next to mine, so that might be nice. We can all hang out."

"I'll never have a chance to seduce you again, will I?" I say, teasing her. "I've got a roommate who keeps pink and purple bedding on my bed, and you're neighbors with my cousin. Oi. Grace, I'm still gonna do my best but you're gonna have to help me figure this out."

"Well, I *do* just so happen to know Brittany's class and cheerleading schedule, so..."

"A great help already! I knew I could count on my future wife."

"Shush, you!"

"Only if you kiss me."

"Don't tempt me!"

"I'll tempt you every day for the rest of your life."

"Promise?"

"Promise."

WANT **FREE** exclusive bonus flash forward scenes starring Dare and Grace? Sign up to check those out here:

Dirty Irish Summer (Summer Break Epilogue)

VALENTINE'S AND CHILL (TEASER)

Cupid has a wicked sense of humor.

A perfect match! That's what the email said.

Seriously.

Our college matched us up. World's silliest V-Day experiment.

We both rolled our eyes.

You were too damn perfect and I was the playboy bad boy your mother warned you about.

Then I saw you the second time. At the airport. Arguing over a cancelled flight.

You saw me before the ticket agent could finish saying *blizzard*.

A perfect match. Remember? Is that why you're staring, cute lips parted into a delicious little O?

Like you can't decide whether you want to kiss me or rip my head off?

Let's have some fun pretend that stupid survey was 100% accurate.

Flights may be cancelled, baby, but Valentine's Day has just begun.

You're **MINE**.

ALLY

Cancelled.
Cancelled, cancelled, cancelled.

Every single flight today has been cancelled. I stare up at the angry, bright red words next to each and every flight number on the information screen. A little part of me hopes that maybe it's some kind of joke. Like April Fool's, right? Haha! Jokes on you, Ally. You fell for it.

It's not April Fool's Day, though. It's Valentine's. Valentine's Day is basically cancelled.

Not that I had a date for it. I mean, I had plans. Flight plans. But, you know, those are cancelled, so...

"Can I help you?" the woman behind the information desk asks. She's the only other person here.

Yes, I'm *that* person right now. The one who shows up at

the airport when her flight is cancelled, magically expecting it to... *not* be cancelled. What, that's not how this works?

To be fair, I didn't know it was cancelled before I got here. Really now, there's only two feet of snow outside and it took my Uber three times as long to drive here because the roads were so bad, but I thought that by showing up extra early I was being responsible.

"Um, yes, I was wondering if I could get on another flight?" I ask her.

"I can certainly look into that for you, hun, but you should have received an email, too."

"Sorry. I get a lot of emails," I say, hoping she believes my excuse.

"It happens!" she says, far too cheery, a bright smile plastered on her face. "Can I see your ticket, hun?"

I hand over my boarding pass and she scours it for my flight number, taps away at her keyboard, and brings something up on the screen that only she can see.

"Oh, you're in luck!" she says, handing back my boarding pass. "I can get you on a flight tomorrow just before noon. How's 11:40am sound?"

"Um, what?" I ask, blinking fast. "There's nothing earlier?"

"I'm surprised there's one for tomorrow morning, actually," she adds. "They told us to expect cancellations to continue through tomorrow. It's a really bad storm out there. Doesn't happen too often in February but you know how it is."

No, I do not. I feel like I probably should but... for Valentine's Day?

"So... what do I do until then?" I ask. "I kind of have to get back to college."

"Did you come back home for a visit?" she asks. "You could go home until tomorrow. I can print you something out saying your flight was cancelled, and you can show that to an administrator at your school. They should accept it as a valid excuse if you need one for whatever reason."

Yeah, about that...

I'm not going to start explaining everything to some random information desk person, but I kind of sort of decided to travel on my own for the weekend as a spur of the moment thing because it seemed like a good idea at the time? I mean, everyone else has Valentine's Day, and that's great. Boyfriends and girlfriends and love is in the air and I'm sure Cupid is awesome, but...

I have me. I mean, I'm usually my favorite person, so I like myself well enough, but I'm not sure anyone else would understand. Plus, you know, I'm a broke college student. I could barely afford this trip as it is, but I made it work, and now I am definitely not making it work because I really don't have the money to stay in a hotel room overnight, especially considering I'm sure they're booked full since everyone else probably had the better idea of not even trying to go to the airport and stayed at a hotel instead.

Basically I'm really good at school but really bad at airplanes.

"Um, so... is there any way I can get a voucher or something?" I ask. "For a hotel room?"

"Sorry, I wish I could," she says with a shrug that's far too cheery for the words coming out of her mouth. "It's a weather-related cancellation, which isn't covered under the cancellation policy since it's not something we have control over."

"So where am I supposed to stay?" I ask, my voice rising steadily.

"You can sleep in the airport?" she offers.

"What, like on a chair next to my gate?"

"Right!" she says, nodding excitedly. "Except, oh wait, I don't know what gate you are yet. They should figure that out a few hours before your flight. Actually, let me print you out a boarding pass now before I forget. The exciting part is you can go to whatever gate you want for now and find the best seat. You've already gone through security, so you're good to go there. Just don't go back out. They shut down for the night and you won't be able to get back in. But, lucky you, there aren't very many people here right now so you should have your pick of wherever you want."

"Are you being serious right now?" I ask while she prints out my new boarding pass, oblivious. "Seriously, is this... are you... are you serious?"

Yes, this isn't my best and brightest moment ever. I'm angry! I don't want to sleep in an airport chair or on some bench or whatever. I don't want to sleep in an airport at all!

"Here you go, hun!" she says, completely ignoring my outrage as she hands me my new ticket. "You have a great night, alright?"

I want to say something, but before I can, she promptly picks up a sign that says, "Sorry we missed you. Come back during normal operating hours," and then walks away, leaving me stranded and alone in the middle of the airport.

I blink, standing there for a second, confused as to what just happened.

Then I turn around, look up, and everything bad in the world gets even worse.

"You..." I say, staring at the absolute last person I ever expected to see here.

"Hey Ally," he says, smirking at me, his eyes glancing up and down, checking me out. "Did you know we're a perfect match?"

JAMES

oday I met my perfect match.

Seriously, that's what the subject of the email my college sent me said. Silliest Valentine's Day experiment or what?

The Statistics Social Club, or SSC--because, yeah, obviously that should be a thing--decided to do some social experiment where they hounded every single person on campus to fill out this survey so they could be matched.

"Dude, James, you could find your perfect match," my friend, Ed, told me.

Yes, I have friends in the SSC. Look, I'm not going to judge someone just because they have an intense fascination with statistics. It's a social club, too. They have parties and do math and the parties are cool but I could do without the math part, personally.

At any rate, Ed begged me to fill out the survey, and after

he'd asked me five times I finally caved and did the damn thing.

"Is this really necessary?" I asked him, pointing to one question as he stood over my shoulder.

"You'd be surprised how much you can tell about a person by which kind of cute cat pictures they like," Ed replied with a curt nod.

So, yeah, I picked the cutest fucking cat picture there. You can't even try and tell me that the other pictures were cuter. The one I picked was the cutest, with a dopey looking Siamese cat with a black patch of fur that looked like a half-mustache. He was laying on a cat bed with his adorable little paws curled up like he was about to get into the cutest boxing match ever.

Cutest fucking cat, I'm telling you.

And that's how that started. It ended with me receiving an email telling me I met my perfect match.

Or, you know, I haven't *met* her yet. Her name is Ally. Also, what the fuck, Ed? This isn't perfect. It says we're 99.7% compatible.

You know where the final 0.3% went wrong? She picked a different cute cat picture.

I don't see this relationship going very far, Ally. It's not me, it's you. Yes, that picture of a black and white kitten is cute, but the cutest? You really think so? I question your taste in cute cat pictures. Kittens are cute by default. You have to take points off for that. You don't know if they'll be cute forever.

Cute adult cats is where it's at. They aren't getting less

cute. They were cute, are cute, and will continue to be cute. Hence, the cutest. It's an undeniable fact.

Ally's pretty cute herself, though. I wouldn't mind being her perfect match. I guess we have a lot in common, or so says the stats. Who am I to argue with math?

A few minutes after I meet my perfect match via email, I get another email telling me my flight's been cancelled.

Well, fuck.

I needed that flight.

How am I supposed to get back to college?

How am I supposed to complain to Ed in person that Ally can't be my perfect match because she has some seriously questionable logic regarding the cutest cat?

Come on, Ed. You need to weigh those stats a little more heavily. Algorithms or something. Fuck if I know. I'm not the statistician here. You're in the damn stats club, Ed!

Cancelled flight should probably mean I should stay where I am, but I never liked doing what I'm supposed to do. Plus, I like airports. There's a lot you can do in an airport. Some people hate them, but they just don't realize all the cool shit that you can do in one if you figure things out ahead of time.

Do you know how much cool shit I can do if I have the airport all to myself?

Man, I am living the dream over here. Aw yeah.

So I pack. I go to the airport. I get through security. I'll figure out my ticket home once I'm in.

I head to the airline information desk to do exactly that and...

She gapes at me, her cute little heart-shaped lips blossoming into the most delicious looking O.

Fuck.

I'm starting to reconsider this perfect match thing. Maybe her opinion on cute cats isn't that important.

And those eyes. She's got these subtly sexy bedroom eyes that she accents with a faint hint of smoky eyeshadow. Ally's got a lot to like, actually. The picture from our perfect match email looked nice, but I'm not sure any picture could really do her justice. She's made to be viewed in motion. Stillness doesn't suit her at all.

"You--" she says, hesitating.

"Hey, Ally. Did you know we're a perfect match?"

WANT to read the rest of **Valentine's and Chill**, starring James and Ally? Go check out their story here!

Valentine's and Chill

A NOTE FROM MIA

Make sure you don't miss any of my new releases by signing up for my VIP readers list!

Cherrylily.com/Mia

You can also find me on Facebook for more sneak peeks and updates here:

Facebook.com/MiaClarkWrites

You can find all of my books on Amazon, including my bestselling Stepbrother With Benefits series!

All of Mia Clark's Books

Thanks so much for reading Dare and Grace's story!

Honestly, they were a ton of fun to write, and their story was something I've always wanted to write about. It might seem kind of crazy to go travel alone and then wind up on dates with someone, but I think that's what makes it a fun sort of fantasy to think about, you know?

Admittedly, I have also occasionally gone on dates with men in other countries when I'm traveling solo, so...

I don't want to say that Dare and Grace's story was based off of anything or anyone in particular, but I may or may not been inspired to write this based off of a date or two I went on once or twice, haha. I'll keep that one a secret. Shh! Don't tell anyone.

What I like about "travel romance" is that it's fun to explore new and exciting things. That's mostly what this story was about for me. Grace is trapped in her ways, stuck being the good girl that everyone expects her to be, but what if she wants to let loose now and then?

Well... Dare Mackenzie is very good at letting loose, but he's not as much of a bad boy as some. They'll definitely get in trouble together, but it'll be a good and fun sort of trouble, I think.

There's definitely something to be said for the really bad boy or the alpha-hole or whatever you want to call it, but I wanted this story to be more about exploring something new in a place that's completely different and finding something really special there. And then figuring out what can come of it if you let yourself be open to the possibilities.

You never know, right?

This was originally planned as a quicker St. Patrick's Day sort of story, but if I'm being honest it kind of got away from me and turned into something more. I wanted to leave it with an ending that made it obvious that Dare and Grace are together, but I also wanted to consider the possibility of writing more stories about them in the future, too.

I'm working on an epilogue, though! I may be done it by the time you're reading this. The link to the epilogue before this, and the one I'll include at the end of this note, will either go to the free epilogue or else you can sign up to receive first notice for when the epilogue is available!

Forewarning, even with an epilogue I reserve the right to write more of Dare and Grace in the future, haha. Look, they're going to have a happily ever after, but I think it's fun to see what they do before then, after then, and everything everywhere in between.

I tend to fall in love with my characters and want to write more and more of them sometimes, which you may have noticed with the inclusion of Brittany and the mention of Caleb (and Scarlet) at the end...

Which, speaking of, I will be working on Brittany's story at some point. Hers will be a bit more dramatic and intense at some points, with a little bit of a villain vibe happening and a hero to come save her (or help her save herself). I'm excited for that one and I hope you'll check it out, too! I'd like to include Dare and Grace in that one, along with all of the other characters I write that I know you love.

I really like tying all my stories together, haha. Just a friends in college, new adult, forbidden romance sort of vibe in a lot of different ways, you know? It's fun!

I definitely hope you loved Dare and Grace's story, and I hope you love all of my characters in their own way. If you're new to my books, go check out more! If you want to start at the absolute beginning, I recommend Stepbrother With Benefits, but I've got something for everyone, shorter, longer, more taboo, less, and so on, so I'm sure you'll find something that you're into.

I still recommend Stepbrother With Benefits 1 first though, haha. Ethan and Ashley get into some crazy adventures together and they were the start of this whole wild world.

I'd love if you could leave a review for Dare and Grace's story, too! I like seeing what you think and knowing what you like so I can write more of it in the future.

What did you think of Grace and Dare meeting like that in Dublin? Was it completely by chance, or maybe Dare noticed her from afar and was coming to talk to her before she almost toppled into the river? Hm...

Did you like the whole Dublin setting? Would you like to read more stories that take place in different countries? Big cities, small towns, or something else entirely?

And... was it worth the wait for Dare and Grace to get all steamed up in her hotel room? Those were my favorite parts, but mostly because I felt like they were teasing and tormenting each other all day that they had a lot of sexual tension to let out on each other, haha. Fun times, that.

I'd love to hear your thoughts, though! Let me know what you think.

Thanks so much for reading. I really appreciate it!

~Mia

P.S. If you haven't read any of my books before, I highly recommend starting with my **Stepbrother With Benefits** series. You can start out slow to see what you think and then really dig your teeth into it if you love what you're reading. Ethan and Ashley are a ton of fun together. I know you're going to love them!

Stepbrother With Benefits 1

If you're looking for something similar to Dare and Grace's story though, definitely check out James and Ally in Valentine's and Chill. Their story of getting trapped in an airport during a blizzard on Valentine's Day is super fun with silly flirty banter and a whole lot of steaminess once they finally admit they're into each other. I like them a lot, too.

Valentine's and Chill

ABOUT THE AUTHOR

Mia likes to have fun in all aspects of her life. Whether she's out enjoying the beautiful weather or spending time at home reading a book, a smile is never far from her face. She's prone to randomly laughing at nothing in particular except for whatever idea amuses her at any given moment.

Sometimes you just need to enjoy life, right?

She loves to read, dance, and explore outdoors. Chamomile tea and bubble baths are two of her favorite things. Flowers are especially nice, and she could get lost in a garden if it's big enough and no one's around to remind her that there are other things to do.

She lives in New Hampshire, where the weather is beautiful and the autumn colors are amazing.

You can find the rest of her books (here)

You can also email her any time at Mia@Cherrylily.com if you have questions, comments, or if you'd just like to say hi!

Made in the USA
San Bernardino, CA
22 January 2020